Praise for

The Ethical Assassin

In this, his first novel, Dr. William Ferraiolo brings us a damaged hero stumbling through the ruins of his once perfect life, who has chosen murder as his path instead of making sense of the causes of his destruction, a path that takes us through the deepest, darkest woods of the mind.

Tim McGarvey, author of *Only the Days We Danced*

T0348669

The Ethical Assassin

A Vigilante's Memoir

Editor's Note

The text of this book is taken from a leather-bound journal found lying on a table at a diner in Sonora, California. At the owner's request, the name of the diner is not included here. There is no indication as to the identity of the author, apart from a vague description offered by the waitress who found the book and waited on the man who, apparently, left it along with his payment for breakfast (and left a significant tip as well). That man, according to the description offered, is a tall, white male around the age of sixty. He is also described as being very polite and soft-spoken. At the time, the man wore a full, salt-and-pepper beard, and he was either fully bald, or he shaved his head. Beyond this, there is no further description of the presumed author of the memoir contained in these pages.

This book is published without any claim regarding its authenticity. The events described herein may have occurred, or they may be invented to some degree or other. They may be *entirely* fictitious. Researchers have been unable to determine the accuracy of the general account offered in these pages or of the specific crimes mentioned herein. This *might* be a true story. The *title* was provided by the author. It was written on the first page of the journal. The text has been edited only insofar as grammar, punctuation, spelling, and general structure are concerned. The *substance* of the text is entirely attributable to the unknown author. Anyone with information about the crimes alleged and described in this journal is encouraged to contact the relevant legal authorities. The killer (if he *is* a killer) is, as far as anyone knows, still at large.

The Ethical Assassin

A Vigilante's Memoir

William Ferraiolo

ROUNDFIRE
BOOKS

London, UK
Washington, DC, USA

CollectiveInk

First published by Roundfire Books, 2025
Roundfire Books is an imprint of Collective Ink Ltd.,
Unit 11, Shepperton House, 89 Shepperton Road, London, N1 3DF
office@collectiveinkbooks.com
www.collectiveinkbooks.com
www.roundfire-books.com

For distributor details and how to order please visit the 'Ordering' section on our website.

ISBN: 978 1 80341 769 1
978 1 80341 770 7 (ebook)
Library of Congress Control Number: 2024933332

A CIP catalogue record for this book is available from the British Library.

Design: Lapiz Digital Services

UK: Printed and bound by CPI Group (UK) Ltd, Croydon, CR0 4YY
Printed in North America by CPI GPS partners

We operate a distinctive and ethical publishing philosophy in all areas of our business, from our global network of authors to production and worldwide distribution.

For My Victims

The Ethical Assassin's Story

What I Do

I only kill people who *deserve* to die. That is *my* judgment about these people because of what *they* have done to harm the innocent. If anyone else ever reads this account, then the reader must render an independent verdict regarding the people I mention here. Presumably, the reader will also render judgment about the author as well. Those opinions on the part of the reader are *not* up to me. Very little is, ultimately, up to me.

Hopefully, my assessment of the people I have killed is correct or, at the very least, morally *defensible*. This is, at any rate, what I *tell* myself. In this way, I practice my new life's purpose, as I understand it. I *hope* that there is *something* worthwhile in what I have done. It is hard to know whether I have been in the right or in the wrong regarding the crimes I describe here. After reading this memoir, some may conclude that I *also* deserve to die. Perhaps *they* are correct. Who am I to judge such matters, after all? I am just another talking primate among billions of others on this planet. I have killed a few of the other talking primates, but my assassinations are not very numerous yet, and I may be caught and imprisoned or have killed myself before I can end many more lives. So far, I have been *lucky* where killing other people is concerned, I suppose.

Time will tell.

Though I *hope* that I am an *ethical* assassin, it may be that I have done things that should *not* have been done. A man can only know so much, after all. While I am able, however, I *may* continue to kill people who, in my judgment, *need* killing. At the time of this writing, I am undecided as to whether or not I am *done* killing. I certainly keep meeting people who, in my judgment, *need* killing. Obviously, I do not kill *all* of them. That would be an enormous undertaking, and it almost certainly would have gotten me killed or captured by now. Some of the people who need killing continue to breathe both in and out. They continue to do terrible things. To me, it seems that such people can be found just about *everywhere*.

Is there anyone who really *disagrees* that *some* people *need* killing? Do most parents *disagree* that a man who *raped* and murdered their *children* would *need* killing? Do the perpetrators of genocide *not* need killing? Do child traffickers *not* need killing? It is difficult for me to believe that anyone *really* disagrees here. People *do*, however, *say* that they disagree. I have heard people claim that "no human being deserves to die," in those exact words, as well as in other terms that amount to the same thing. It is *impossible* for me to take these people and their claims *seriously*. I cannot help but wonder if they have actually *met* many human beings or paid any attention to current events, or learned anything about the history of the human race. *Mao* did *not* deserve to die? Stalin and Hitler did *not* deserve to be killed? Those guys *were* human beings, were they not?

There are *millions* of "lesser" destroyers out there as well. They cannot match history's greatest mass murderers in terms of the *number* of lives that they destroy, but that is due to limitations on their abilities. It is *not* because they are less evil than the genocidal maniacs who periodically seize political power. The "little" villains simply lack the *capacity* to kill and torture millions because they do not run nations or have access to militaries and storm troopers willing to obey their commands. They are *small* people. Their reach is limited. Though they cannot perpetrate evil deeds on a societal or international scale, does anyone really doubt that they *would* if they could? People who intentionally destroy *children* are not prevented from destroying whole societies by their *consciences*, after all. No, I *reject* the proposition that *no* human being *needs* to be killed. I reject it so thoroughly that I have taken it upon myself to remove some of the worst people I have encountered from the company of the rest of those who walk the face of this planet. I *have* killed people who *needed* killing.

Contemplating this as something like a *calling* is part of what I *do* now. This *might* be my calling. I *may* have found a viable *purpose* for my life. Then again, I may have suffered something like a psychotic break. Surely, some psychiatrists would diagnose me as mentally ill, and as suffering from some form of dysfunction or other. How could an *honest* murderer simply reject such a diagnosis out of hand? When a guy starts killing people, it is at least *possible* that something has gone wrong with that guy's brain. Then again, it may just be that some people really do *need* killing, and our culture has simply gone squeamish about admitting that this is so. *That* is also a possibility worth considering, is it not? I wonder how many innocent people have been killed and caused to suffer needlessly as a result of our culture's irrational "tolerance" of hideous people and their nefarious deeds. *Somebody* has to do something about *some* of it, at the *very* least. I have done something. Perhaps others might do *their* part as well.

Time will tell.

It is notoriously difficult to know and understand *oneself* and the *true* motives behind one's own behavior. I will not claim that what I have done, and what I describe in these pages, is *virtuous* or admirable in *any* way. Presenting myself as a moral exemplar is *not* a project that appeals to me. Nobody should *hope* to become what I have become. It is a fairly *uncomfortable* existence. I will not even insist that I am *not* mentally ill. Many crazy people do not *know* that they are crazy, after all. How can I know such things with anything approaching certainty, or even with a high degree of confidence? All of us struggle with confusion, reservations, challenges, and half-blind efforts to find lives that are worth living. Insanity is something of a sliding scale, it seems. Everybody "gets a little crazy" now and again, do they not? In this way, I suppose I am very much like just about everybody else I encounter. Most of the other people with whom I interact have probably *not* killed as many people as I have killed. Most people have not killed *anybody*, as far as I am aware. This is probably as it should be. People have different interests, do they not? Not everybody is going to be *good* at killing terrible people. Not everybody is going to derive a sense of satisfaction from doing the kind of things that I have done. I *hope* not, anyway.

Everybody needs a *reason* to get up in the morning, though. My family *was* that reason before my "new life" began. I loved my family more than I loved anything else in this world. Most people could probably say the same thing about their relationship to their families. Good for them. People *should* love their families (mostly). What happens to such people when the beloved family *disappears*? Well, I cannot speak for anyone *else*. In *my* case, the sudden loss of my entire family led, in conjunction with other events, to my decision to start killing some people who, in my estimation, *needed* killing. So, evidently, that is *one* possible result of the devastating loss of one's family. There are, to be sure, more *muted* responses available. To each his own, I guess.

One day, I woke up and realized that *my* reason for getting up in the morning had been stripped away. It happened, more or less, all at once. There is more to say about that, and I will get to it at some point, but there is also more to my story than the loss of my family. There is always more to *every* story than the part that gets told or written down. For example, I have discovered many re-emerging memories that were once quite vague and indistinct to me. Some of these memories are now *very* clear and obtrusive, and this change has emerged after my family no longer exerted quite the same hold on my attention as when they were still alive and with me. I cannot seem to push the re-emergent memories away to the nether regions of my mind.

4

They *insist* upon themselves. They refuse to be forgotten again. Good for them. I am grateful for these memories re-introducing themselves to me. I value them. What are *any* of us without our memories?

Something in me, it now seems, had been waiting quietly beneath the surface layer of the typical concerns about the family, the occupation, the friendly get-togethers, and all of the other trappings of a "regular" life among others in 21st Century United States. I was a *normal* guy, to all appearances. Only *after* my family ceased to be my primary concern did I begin to notice some habits of thought that had always been customary for me, but that had never erupted into actions like those I have indulged in after the bonds of basic civility and custom fell away. Some of these tendencies feel as if they run *very* deep in me. As far as I can tell, they have *always* been there. It seems that I have been, in some sense, "preparing" for a day when "the rules" ceased to mean anything to me. This may have been happening at a subconscious level. I cannot know for certain. That is one of the features of the subconscious. It is difficult to be entirely aware of what may be going on at that level of cognition. Indeed, most of what the mind is doing may be inaccessible to the consciousness. We can know and understand ourselves only partially at best. Each of us is, I suspect, a little mysterious.

Even as a child, it is now clear to me, I paid attention to things that my friends did not seem to notice, or things that meant nothing to most of the people in any room in which I found myself. As a child, I was surprisingly *vigilant*, I now realize. Perhaps I have something like a "sixth sense," and it is more attuned to threats and dangers than most people can manage. Then again, maybe everyone has this faculty, but most do not pay heed to it in the way that I always have. How can I know the minds of others with that kind of specificity, after all?

I only know so much about what my *own* mind is doing. I am, however, aware of *some* of it.

I have almost *never*, for example, entered a room without noticing every exit and every object that could potentially be used as a weapon if need be. This is a long-standing habit of observation for me. Sitting with my back to the door has always made me extraordinarily uncomfortable, and I generally work to avoid finding myself in a place that does not allow me to observe the entrance to the room and the majority of the people in my immediate environment. I am uneasy if I cannot see everything around me that could potentially become a threat. I pay attention.

Even in grade school, I always tried to sit in the back corner furthest from the classroom door, not because I wanted to misbehave without the teacher seeing me, but because I wanted to be able to observe *everyone* in the classroom, and anyone who might enter. It was important to me to be prepared to be the *first* to respond to any potential danger or disruption. *Something* might happen. *Someone* had to be prepared for *whatever* might be coming. I generally positioned myself like a security guard in the classroom and at recess, and I watched the playground as if someone had ordered me to be on the lookout for any trouble that might arise. What the other little kids did to each other was not my primary concern. Some greater danger seemed always just over the horizon, from my perspective. I always stayed prepared for *something*.

Even as a fairly young child in school, I always identified potential threats and always knew where to get my hands on the heaviest and sharpest objects in any room. Nobody was going to "get me" without a fight, and I was ready to protect others as well, if need be. I learned how to spot the bully in any classroom, and the bullies generally seemed to sense that they should not try to pick on *me*. Well, the bullies never tried me more than *one* time, at any rate.

These memories once seemed much more distant to me than they do now. This is *odd*, is it not? Memories tend to *fade* over time. The more distant the memory, the less clear and distinct it is, for the most part. Memories of my youthful attentiveness, however, are far more urgent to me today than they were just a few years ago. Now, I recall my sustained vigilance quite readily and very clearly. I even remember other kids occasionally looking to me for protection at various times about which I had completely forgotten for many years. They sensed that I was prepared in some way that they were not. People often seem to perceive that there is someone else paying attention in a way that is protective or attuned to potential trouble, even when there are no real signs, to the untrained and less-than-vigilant eye, that trouble is brewing. I was *always* the kid paying attention in that particular way. Evidently, I am still the guy paying attention in that way. I suppose most of us do not change in terms of the most fundamental features of our character or our behavioral tendencies. I think I always have probably been, in some sense, what I am today. I *could* be mistaken, of course. Perhaps my memories are playing tricks on me these days.

Even today, I am *always* paying attention. Nobody who looks potentially dangerous or possibly in the process of trying to "get away with something" escapes my notice for very long. I feel compelled to "be on the lookout" at all times. It is actually pretty taxing on my mental energies, but I am willing to make the trade of somewhat heightened anxiety or worry, if that is what is needed for constant vigilance. Especially in public places, I am always in a condition of hyper-readiness. Some may regard this as an unhealthy habit of mind. Those people are *wrong*. The world is a dangerous place, and nobody gets out alive. I am sure I have *read* that *somewhere*. Carelessness is, in my view, inexcusable for adults. Carelessness is apt to get people killed. I should know. I have killed some people who were guilty of carelessness, as well as guilty of particularly heinous crimes. *Those* people really ought to be more careful. Those who do horrible things ought to consider the possibility that they will suffer the consequences of their actions. Luckily, many of them seem to be fairly oblivious regarding potential consequences. That comes in handy for me.

Perhaps a moment of carelessness will be *my* undoing one day. Nobody is perfect, after all. Even someone as vigilant as me can fail to notice some danger or other, and end up suffering for it in some unanticipated fashion. Perhaps my story will end in prison. I do *not* want to go to prison, but neither do most of those who find themselves there, I suppose. I might end up where I do *not* want to be.

Time will tell.

Wile E. Coyote

I was, to all appearances, an extraordinarily *ordinary* guy for *many* years. My family, my job, and the place I lived were the stuff of, to use an admittedly hackneyed phrase, a Norman Rockwell painting. Sitcom dads are fairly similar to my former self (although I was never particularly funny). I had a wife and two children whom I supported in, more or less, the usual way. There was one son and one daughter in my family. Statistically, I was strikingly *average*. I managed to provide my family with a house, food, insurance, two vehicles, private school, and most of the stuff that most Americans generally regard as necessities or as instruments for attaining something like normalcy or stability. I was a husband and father. *That* was my primary identity. Now, I am neither of those things. Does a father and husband continue to *be* a husband and father when his wife and children all die simultaneously? That simply *cannot* be the truth of things. A husband *must* have a wife and a father *must* have children (preferably *living* children). *Dead* children, I can regrettably report, are just *not* the same feature of one's "family life" as are living children. I do not *feel* like much of a father these days.

The office in which I performed most of my occupational duties was also quite average in every respect that anyone might have noticed. It was neither large nor small. There was nothing impressive about the thing. It was not the "corner office" that so many seem to covet for reasons that, frankly, escape me. My professional responsibilities were neither insignificant nor fabulously important. I was a functionary. I was a factotum. I was a cog in a complex assemblage of interlocking wheels keeping "the machine" running. That was just fine with me. It put food on the table. It paid the mortgage. It provided health insurance for my family. I did not insist on getting much more than that out of my job.

The company for which I worked is exactly like every other mid-sized corporation of its type, and the industry in which I worked is one of those that has persisted in business across the nation and much of the Western World for well over a hundred years. Probably about one quarter of the people in every mid-sized town in the United States works in the same type of industry, or in one with which this industry is fairly closely associated. Think of an *insurance* company. I did not work in insurance, but my job was "kind of like that" in any respect that anybody might notice. There was a lot of paperwork, pointless meetings, a hierarchy of command, an HR department, and a bunch of employees functioning largely on autopilot. Most of us were just putting food on the table, paying the bills, etc.

With very few exceptions, nobody ever looked twice at me or thought about me if I was not in the room with them. Being a nondescript guy among a bunch of other similarly nondescript people working in a manner that was not particularly interesting was the way that I spent my time during most weekdays. I got a few weeks of vacation time each year. When I was on vacation, I doubt that anyone at my company really noticed. That was *all* fine with me, as far as I knew or cared, or ever bothered to think about my lot in life at the time. I had a family, I had a job, and I was grateful for all of it.

So, I was "doing just fine," and I told people so any time they asked me how things were going. "No complaints," I would almost always say. Also, I almost never actually complained about anything. I was "happy," in the way that people often claim to be "happy" when they are not really thinking about what happiness *means*. My life was much as I had envisioned an adult life was supposed to be. The *past* tense is particularly operative here. My life is *nothing* like that *now*.

We often hear, of course, that "all good things must come to an end," and all good things in *my* life *did* come to an end, and they came to that end *very* abruptly. I could not have been prepared for this abrupt end. Everything that mattered to me disappeared in the space of a *few seconds*. *Everything*. A *few seconds*. *Gone*.

It was literally impossible for me to comprehend this sudden and complete obliteration of the foundations upon which I had been living my entirely "normal" life in habitual and unreflective fashion. To this day, I cannot explain the magnitude of the sudden shift in my understanding of what I thought my life was *supposed* to *be*. Perhaps a more talented writer could do my story justice in a way that is beyond my abilities. I am *not* a talented writer. It is something of a shame that this account is the best that I can manage. Nonetheless, this *is* the best that I can manage. So, the shame is on *me*, I suppose. I can live with that. What, after all, is my alternative? I cannot very well hire a better writer to tell this particular story. Doing so would be ludicrous and extraordinarily unwise. Perhaps, if I end up in prison at some point in the future, a talented writer will come looking for *me*.

Time will tell.

Maybe I went into some form of shock upon learning about what had happened. I do not really understand what "shock" of this nature amounts to, after all. It is not as if I suffered some physical injury and lost too much blood too quickly. I understand (vaguely) what *shock* is when one loses too much blood too quickly. The body goes into a type of distress dysfunction. The organs, including the brain, are deprived of oxygen and other nutrients. Organs can fail under these conditions. Perceptions and cognition falter when one is in shock. *Something* in me faltered, for sure. This was not due to loss of blood, other fluids, or oxygen, at least not as far as I can tell. My *body* was, as far as

I am aware, unchanged in any significant respect. Then again, I am not trained to understand how a disruption to the mind can impact the functioning of the body, and impact the brain in particular. Can the sudden deprivation of *normalcy* lead to similar symptoms as the sudden loss of blood and oxygen to the brain? Blood was lost, to be sure, but it was not lost from *my* body. It was all of the *other* blood that mattered to me that drained away far too quickly for me to be able to process what had happened. *People* disappeared from my life in, from my perspective, an *instant*. The people I loved the most were just *gone*, all at once. For *this*, I was *entirely* unprepared. My youthful vigilance did me *no* good on this occasion.

Is it correct that *psychological* "shock" is something like *physiological* shock due to bodily damage? Does the brain falter in similar fashion? I am not a psychiatrist and, frankly, I am not sure how much I trust pronouncements from that profession in general. Does anyone *fully* trust shrinks? How can *they* be so confident about what goes on in someone *else's* mind? There *has* to be a significant amount of guesswork, or so it seems to me. It is not as if they have direct access to the relevant thoughts and to their processing at various levels of cognition. The shrink gets a description of events, and a recounting of conscious mental states from a patient who may or may not be telling the whole truth of the matter. Indeed, even the patient cannot know the *whole* truth of his own mind at levels unavailable to consciousness. We do not know *ourselves* that well. What can a psychiatrist discern from such unreliable reports about what has gone on in the patient's mind?

Also, the psychiatrists generally seem to find a diagnosis that requires some type of *pharmaceutical* intervention, do they not? That is awfully lucrative for the drug companies, and I have heard and read enough about "benefits" (kickbacks) to prescribers that I am a little suspicious about the real necessity for introducing drugs to the patient. Who knows? Maybe the drugs help. Maybe they save lives. Then again, maybe there is a lot of modern "witch-doctoring" going on in the fields of psychiatry and pharmacology. This is none of my concern, I suppose. If people want the drugs, then they can have as much of them as they want, for all I care. It certainly appears that they *do* get a lot of drugs, in any event. People seem to *love* their pills.

In any case, I have *no* idea how to characterize the change within my own psyche at the moment I heard the news, nor do I know what to say about my state of mind all these years later when I consider everything that happened on that day and the days immediately following. I know that things have changed over the years between that day and this one, *dramatically* from my point of view. Exactly how and when these changes took place is not particularly interesting to me. My life *now* is almost *nothing* like my life *before* I received *the* phone call. *Everything* about which I once cared so deeply was simply *taken* from me at that moment. It did not all disappear a little bit at a time, in a manner that allowed me to adjust *gradually*. What I thought of as my *entire* life just "went away" all at once. I "had it all," and then I had *nothing*, as far as I was concerned. What would *that* do to *any* man? It played a central role, I am fairly confident, in turning *me* into a killer. Of *that*, I am almost grateful on some occasions. At other times, it feels like a corollary injustice or, at the very least, an additional facet of the crushing misfortune of losing my family. If my wife and kids were still alive, then I would probably not endanger them by doing the things I have done since I lost them. As things stand, they are in no danger. They are *safely* dead.

I cannot speak for any man *other* than myself regarding the impact of this type of event. The phone call whereby I learned that my family had all died at once left me feeling like I was suspended in mid-air. I felt like a cartoon character who has run off of a cliff, but not yet fallen because he has *just* looked down. In the Road Runner cartoons, gravity only takes effect when the character looks down to see that he is now standing on *nothing*. Like Wile E. Coyote, I experienced that instant when I realized that the ground had dropped away and there was now nothing but the abyss beneath my feet. I felt the abyss yawning beneath me, but there was no experience of plummeting to the ground. Feeling as if I had touched something beneath me might have been comforting. I felt absolutely nothing beneath me or supporting my body. I just "hung there," suspended above the nothingness where my family had been. Plummeting into the abyss and finally hitting something would have been preferable, I think. That would have felt like *something*, at least.

The coyote in the cartoons falls, crashes, makes sounds like an accordion, re-establishes bodily integrity, as if by magic, and then goes back about the business of trying to chase down the Road Runner. He still has the same *purpose* he always had. He recovers quickly. Cartoon characters can do that. The coyote still *knows* what he is *supposed* to do. His purpose is *written* for him. He has a *script*, after all. Wile E. Coyote exists *only* for the sake of chasing the Road Runner. All of his efforts serve *that* endeavor. He is *lucky* that way. I *envy* him in that way. His "character" is fixed by the script in which he exists. He has no need to try to make sense of his life. He does not struggle to find a *meaning* for his existence. Everything is quite *obvious* for Wile E. Coyote. It must be nice to be a cartoon character existing within the confines of a script in which nobody ever *really* dies.

After the *crash* in *my* life, there was no obvious purpose for me to pursue. Nobody showed me a *script*. There were, to be sure, things that had to be done. Funerals do not organize themselves, after all. I have vague and indistinct memories of phone calls, visits from people who "wanted to help," but who also knew that there was nothing really that they could do about anything other than helping to handle trivial formalities and fairly meaningless rituals. The relevant rituals are intended to be comforting, I suppose. Those rituals are also more lucrative than is decent, are they not? The sickness and death industries are the most reliable sectors of any economy, I suppose. People *die* more consistently than they do just about anything else. The old quip about "death and taxes" is no joke. The death part is a *certainty* indeed.

When the caskets have to be *closed* for an *entire* family, then the whole affair is somewhat *less* comforting, I think. People just show up to "pay their respects" to *boxes* with photographs standing next to them on easels. They do this because they have been taught that they are *supposed* to do this. I did not *need* them to show up. Frankly, I would have preferred to dispense with the whole funeral. Of course, I have *also* been taught what one is supposed to do in such cases. There are cultural customs that *must* be observed, for reasons I simply do not understand. Why can we not leave the *dead* alone, for God's sake? No family member *wants* to attend the funeral and perform the rituals. In any case, I *hope* nobody *wants* that. There is something positively ghoulish about a funeral. The show, however, must go on, I guess.

There can be no dispute about whether the dead *people* are truly *gone* when the caskets are *closed*. Nothing says "gone" quite like a closed box, a photograph, and an expressionless erstwhile husband and father who has just ceased to be anything that *matters* to him anymore. My wife and children were *not* present at the funeral. Their mangled bodies were in those boxes, as far as I was aware anyway. A mangled, lifeless body *cannot* be my wife or child. My family was composed of *living* people. Those living people did not show up at the funeral. Where that left *me* was entirely unclear. What *is* a middle-aged man who, suddenly, no longer has a wife or children? Is there even a *word* for that?

Children who lose their *parents* are *orphans*. A parent who loses his children is nothing-in-particular. There is, to the best of my knowledge, no word for *that* in the English language.

I think I probably still *am* a nothing-in-particular, in many respects. No term is necessary, I guess. A husband who loses his wife is a *widower*, but he is no longer a *husband*, is he? What the *hell* is a *husband* the moment his *wife* dies? When, exactly, does he *stop* being a husband? This is an interesting question that makes precisely *no* difference at the moment it arises in a man's life. No man wonders, at the funeral, "am I still married, or am I now a bachelor?" as he stares at a casket. Well, I *hope* no man wonders about such matters at *that* moment. Who the hell knows what other people may or may not think about at *any* given time? Frankly, I do not care.

Most widowers are old and gray. A man who does not look "old enough" to be a widower, and who has not quite managed to process the loss of his entire family is just some guy standing there shaking hands with people who say things like, "there are no words," and I, at any rate, found myself wondering why everyone insists upon *saying* that there is *nothing* to say. Why *speak* at all? In any case, I found *myself* wondering about the awkward things that people felt compelled to say. If I can ponder semantics and motives at the funeral, then I guess other men *can* wonder if they are still husbands. There is something ludicrous about all of this, is there not?

The human mind is bizarre. Sometimes, it seems like it is disconnected from the body and from the surrounding environment. The human mind is a strange adaptation to evolutionary pressures, or so it seems to me. What is with all the thinking beyond what is necessary for survival and procreation? That is another matter that lies beyond my powers of understanding. Perhaps it is best that things remain that way. I have no need to understand *everything*.

In any case, *my* mind often feels disconnected from *me* these days. It is a difficult condition to describe. I lack the talent to do descriptive justice to the condition in question. Someone else could probably do a better job in this area. I am not, however, someone else. These days, I am just *me*. I am *all* I have these days. Nothing else is left from the life I once lived mostly on autopilot. I *missed* out on much of what should have mattered to me when my family was still alive and kicking. The food needed to get to the table, after all. Somebody had to pay the mortgage and keep a roof over our heads. Otherwise, something terrible might happen. I could not risk *that*, right?

The funeral and the immediate aftermath passed in a blur, as I suppose these things always do. Who *wants* to retain *those* memories? Let them *remain* a blur. I could not have cared less about the papers I had to sign in subsequent days, but that too is apparently part of the ritual that has grown up around the "death industry" in the United States. Somebody has to get *paid* when people *die*, do they not? I signed here and initialed there, as I was instructed to do. Everyone murmured something intended to indicate that they were "sorry for my loss," and that I should call if I *ever* needed *anything*. People who said this mostly hoped that I would never *actually* need anything from *them*, I strongly suspect. It is just the kind of thing that one says on this type of occasion. What else *is* there to be said?

Within a few days after my family was securely in the ground (and what, after all, is more *secure* than a grave?), I could not help but notice that everyone else went back to the "business as usual" of living their lives. What else were *they* supposed to do, after all? *Their* families were *not* dead. They still had all of the old, familiar responsibilities to which they had to attend. They needed to get the food to the table. The rent or the mortgage needed to be paid. Life *does* "go on" for everybody who is not dead, does it not? After a week or so had passed, I *also* went back to work, because I had *no* idea what else to do with myself.

The paperwork, the phone calls, and the other duties of my employment just meant *nothing* to me after the funeral, however. For whom was I still "earning a living" when nobody was left *living* at home but *me*? I just do not need as much food to get to my lonely table for *one*. I no longer cared about the house. Mortgage be damned. The abyss still yawned beneath me, but I am not, as it turns out, Wile E. Coyote. I am not written to be a "super genius," as is Wile E., and I had no desire simply to "get back to business," and back to a life that no longer really interested me in the least. There is no Road Runner for me to chase. A man can never *really* be a life unto himself *alone*, or so I now suspect. It is literally true that "no man is an island" (though that is generally regarded as a *metaphor*), but I certainly felt detached from anything like a "mainland" to which I might have once belonged. My *family* was my "mainland," and it disappeared all at once.

I was *alone* in the world. I was *adrift*. Men without purpose, everyone knows, can become self-destructive and dangerous creatures. Look at *prisoners*. Those who do *not* find some type of *purpose* in captivity generally do not last very long, or they manage to survive largely for the sake of *damaging* others. They become predators and exploiters of the weak. I did not want to become a prisoner, either literally or figuratively. Whether I succeeded in avoiding that figurative fate is anyone's guess. I have, to be sure, done my share of damage. Whether I will ultimately avoid the *literal* fate of becoming a prisoner is yet to be determined.

Time will tell.

So, I needed to find *something* to give me a reason to get out of bed in the morning. I have plenty of food, after all. My career would not be sufficient to take the place of my family. That became clear to me over a fairly brief span of time. I was no longer very good at my job, because I had no motivation to be good at it. Why should I continue to care about my career? I worked to support my *family*. My career had never been a point of pride for me. I worked because I was *supposed* to do so. That was all. It was a way of paying the bills and putting food on the table. Well, it turns out that I do not eat nearly as much as four people once did. There is, distressingly, plenty of food for me *alone*. A single man does not really *need* to maintain a house, does he? The wife and the children need the house. A single man can live just about anywhere. In the years since I lost my family, I *have* lived just about anywhere. In fact, I *still* live nowhere and anywhere.

I stopped caring about the bills and the groceries, and I began looking for some *other* purpose. If I did not find *something* to do with myself, then I was going to end up in prison or in the ground next to my wife and kids. I needed to fashion a worthwhile life, and I had absolutely *no* idea how to go about doing that all on my own. It is up to others to determine whether I *found* a worthwhile life or not. What I have constructed is a life, but it may or may not be worth living. I am not yet certain. Perhaps I will live out the rest of my life and never be certain whether it is or is not worthwhile.

Time will tell.

Easy Ed

Men bereft of purpose, and without access to *women*, are *sad* and *dangerous* creatures indeed. Men who just *do not care* anymore are men with whom nobody should trifle very lightly. It is just too easy to say the wrong thing in their presence. Calamity can ensue. Ed said *very* much the wrong thing in my presence at a time when I was, to say the least, disinclined to tolerate gently the bile that Ed felt the need to spew to a drinking buddy of his. This mistake turned out to be *fatal* for Ed. He will, I strongly suspect, *not* be missed. Even if someone *does* miss him, I honestly do not care. He is gone because I dispatched him, and I am glad that I got rid of him. When all is said and done, those facts are sufficient for me. I am satisfied that I did precisely what I *wanted* to do to Ed. Whether I was or was not justified in killing Ed is a matter of ambivalence, if not full-fledged indifference, to me. I, for one, will *not* miss this guy.

I decided to kill Ed because I overheard him bragging to a pal of his about how Ed's wife knew better than to ever "mouth off" to him again. Ed had, he stated pointedly, taught her a *lesson*. He was clearly pleased with himself over this "accomplishment" within his marriage. The "tough guy" act was even less appealing than I can describe properly in these pages. I do not have the words to do justice to his venom, or to the self-aggrandizement that went along with it. He related an account of beating his wife and their son so badly that the mother of his child could not walk for a week after "learning her place." His voice dripped with *pride* about the beating. He was lucky enough to have a wife and family, and he held forth self-importantly about *torturing* them. This conversation occurred shortly after *my* wife found "her place" in a grave, and my children found "their places" next to her. The story got my attention. Something in me was "activated" as I listened to this boastful account of utterly *repugnant* behavior.

Ed's son, he bragged, also did not attend school that week, because somebody at the school might have noticed his bruises and his split lip. That, evidently, would have been problematic from Ed's perspective. Ed was, in fact, such a prolific and devoted "instructor" that even his infant daughter had learned not to cry at night when her father was trying to sleep. The baby had been conditioned, according to Ed, through the "negative reinforcement" of being strangled into unconsciousness by Ed's own edifying hands. In this way, the family learned to "respect" the *man* of the house. I did not arrive at the same "appreciation" of Ed's manly character. The thought about getting up, smashing my glass against his head, and stomping Ed into a blood pudding on the barroom floor. The urge to do so certainly appeared before my mind. I am glad, however, that I chose a different approach to dealing with this miscreant. It is important to learn to delay one's gratification, is it not? A beating, I suspected, would prove less than satisfying for me. I knew immediately that I was going to *need* more than that. Merely hurting Ed was *not* what I wanted. Without quite fully realizing the full ramifications of my judgment, I issued Ed with the *death* penalty as I sat in that bar. My family was dead. Surely, I could not allow Ed to get away with a *lesser* punishment than the fate my family had suffered. My family was *innocent* (for the most part), and they were in the ground.

I am almost inclined to give Ed a perverse type of "credit" for the "exquisite detail" he included in his account of the beatings of his wife and child. Were it not for the subject matter, I might describe Ed as something of a *raconteur*. He really had a way of weaving a compelling narrative. I will bet that Ed would have made a better writer than me. Unless he has left a bunch of manuscripts in a desk somewhere, the world is going to have to make do without his collected works. His days of telling stories are *over*. His days of doing or saying *anything* at all are over. I managed to "put a period" at the end of his story. Doing so was startlingly *easy*. Perhaps it should be more difficult to kill a man. I can report that it is *not*. Ed was *easy*.

He had no idea, as far as I could tell, that I overheard this entire conversation. Indeed, Ed never actually met me or spoke to me (on purpose or knowingly, at any rate). This came in handy for my purposes later on. The conversation between Ed and his drinking buddy took place over a few beers at a bar some distance from my home. I was seated near enough to follow Ed's recounting of the events he described, and to hear the muted surprise expressed by Ed's pal. I never learned the buddy's name. That is probably for the best, I suppose.

"Holy cow, Ed," the buddy exclaimed at one point, and he chuckled a little. That is how I know Ed's name. Maybe this remark was intended as something like criticism. Then again, it might have been an expression of admiration for the way that a "real man" handled his intransigent family. It was impossible for me to know how to interpret this expression at the time. To this day, I do not know what the drinking buddy meant by saying "holy cow," in response to the story. That is probably also for the best. Delving into the drinking buddy's mind would hardly have been worth my time and effort, or so I suspect.

I never looked up from my scotch and water (no ice). I carefully betrayed no sign that I was aware of anything apart from my own lonely experience of a Friday night at a dive bar, surrounded by complete strangers. I have never been much of a drinker, but I indulge on the odd occasion. For example, it seems that I am inclined to drink a bit in the aftermath of the sudden destruction of my entire family. I suppose I am *weak* in that way. So be it. We all have our demons and our frailties, do we not? I drank that night, but I did not drink a great deal. Ed's story was more compelling to me than inebriation.

In any event, Ed had caught me on a *very* bad night. I had *buried* my wife and children not too long before I overheard Ed bragging about *beating* the hell out of *his* wife and children. On any other night, I probably would not have been eavesdropping on a conversation between two strangers sitting three empty barstools away from me. I probably would not have been in *any* bar at all. I would have been home with my family. That night, however, I was staring into my drink like a man who had just lost everything he cared about to a car accident. I will get back to that later. *That* night, I had *nothing* else to do with myself. Ed, however, *gave me* something new to do with myself. He hurled it to me like a life preserver thrown to a drowning man. My "life preserver" was a new *reason* to get up in the morning. Ed *needed* killing. An adrenaline rush swept through me when I became aware that I had decided to give Ed exactly what he needed. *This* was something for me to do with myself.

I knew this as clearly as I had ever known *anything* about what I wanted to do to another human being, particularly one "I did not know from Adam," as the expression goes. Even if Ed had *invented* the entire story, which strikes me as unlikely, he *still* needed to die. *My* family was in the ground, after all. Here Ed was, *bragging* about *torturing* his wife and children. I *believed* every word he said. It all had "the ring of truth" about it. If it was not *all* true, then it was still the invention of a genuinely sick and twisted mind that needed to be extinguished. That mind would do more harm than good in this world. How could it be otherwise? Of course, that was not really my primary interest in Ed.

I kept listening, and kept staring blankly into my scotch and water (*still* no ice). I could not have stopped listening if I had *wanted* to stop listening. Ed's story was simply *riveting* to me on that occasion. Also, I had no *reason* to want to stop. Was I being *impolite* by eavesdropping? Well, I was not obsessed with observing propriety in that manner on the night in question. My civility had atrophied a bit in the absence of daily interpersonal interactions with my wife and kids. I guess my family being annihilated caused me to be a little irritable. Again, it seems that I am just weak in that way. Sue me.

Ed continued talking. People like him *always* do it seems. After a brief lull in their conversation, Ed mentioned that he was going fishing the next day. It was going to be Saturday, after all. Weekends are *made* for fishing. There was very little by way of a segue from the one topic to the other. Nothing special had happened, as far as Ed was concerned, after all. Why *not* go and catch a few steelhead trout or whatever other fish he could pull out of the water? Ed named a nearby river, and described the location of his favorite "honey hole," where he had taken fish from the river for years. He also mentioned an old bridge crossing the river right near his favorite fishing spot, and not too far from another distinguishing feature of the area that I decline to describe here. I have no desire to go to prison, after all, and I prefer to avoid leaving *too* many clues regarding the specific places described in these pages. I am not a masochist. Prison may be in my future, but there are no guarantees about that, as far as I know.

Time will tell.

The spot Ed mentioned is pretty hard to miss, for anyone aware of what Ed and I then *both* knew about the bridge and the rest of the area. Ed mentioned that he intended to get an early start on Saturday morning. I decided to get up even *earlier* than Ed that Saturday. In fact, I ended up not sleeping at all. To this day, I do not know Ed's last name. I have never been interested in learning his name. It is splendidly irrelevant to me. No news story about his death has ever presented itself to me, and I have not gone looking for one. His full name is a matter of no consequence to me. Maybe I will learn Ed's surname the hard way. Nevertheless, I still do not know his last name as I write these words.

Time will tell.

My First Kill

Ed and I *never* exchanged words. He never saw me at the river that Saturday. I certainly saw *him*. He was fishing *alone* that morning. Good for him. He was an independent spirit. That was all the opportunity I needed. To this day, I think of Ed being alone as a stroke of good luck for *me*. Perhaps it was something more than mere luck. *Serendipity*, perhaps? Who knows. Whether there is or is not a "grand scheme" is a topic to which I will return later.

If his drinking buddy had joined him that morning, then Ed might still be alive today. *That* would be a shame. As it happens, Ed is dead. I have never felt the slightest pang of regret or moral compunction about what I did to him. What that says about me is not for me to say. Others will judge as they see fit, I suppose. I am here and Ed is gone. That works for me just fine.

There was no blood. I used a tire thumper that I kept in the driver's side door of my car. It is a blunt instrument about two feet long. Truckers evidently use these kinds of clubs to check tire pressure on their vehicles. I did not use it as it was *designed* to be used, I suppose. The thing is heavy for a two-foot-long piece of hardwood. It is *very* solid. I have slammed it repeatedly against a few different trees, and the trees sustained more damage than the tire thumper. It proved very effective for my purpose. I still have it, by the way. I still keep it in my driver's side door. Where else should I keep the thing? I *could*, of course, get rid of it, but *why*? We should respect an effective and well-crafted tool, should we not? I was careful to clean it thoroughly after I was done using it on this occasion. Who would want Ed's DNA on their stuff?

Ed was watching his line in the river. He was paying attention, but not, as it turns out, to the most important elements of his immediate environment. Many people make that mistake, as far as I can tell. Forgive me if I decline to name the river here, but that would be unwise. Someone *might* read this.

Ed never saw or heard me. The bank of the river near the base of the old bridge was all soft, damp soil. It was easy to move quietly. Also, I only needed to take *one* step away from the concrete base of the stairs leading up to the bridge that Ed had mentioned the Friday night before I killed him. That one step brought me into perfect striking distance for the tire thumper. I could not have lined things up better with months of planning. As it happens, all of my "planning" took less than twelve hours, a short drive, and the good fortune that Ed was all alone that Saturday morning. He may as well have been all alone in the *world* at that moment. After all, I *am* all alone in the world. *That* is one of the main reasons that Ed is dead.

Having the tire thumper in my door does not even count as part of any *plan*. It is *always* there. One never knows when a bludgeon might come in handy. With the implement in hand, I took one quick step and slammed the blunt object into the side of Ed's head with all of the force I could muster. I am not a physically small man. That single blow was all that was necessary to drop Ed like a lifeless sack of flesh and bones. Homerun hitters in baseball sometimes describe making perfect contact with a pitch as "swinging straight through the ball" like it is not even there. They say that they do not *feel* the contact when they catch a ball perfectly. I do not recall feeling the contact between the tire thumper and Ed's skull. It felt like he was not even there. I swung "straight through" him. Ed's skull could have been a baseball that I caught with perfect timing from the batter's box. There was something strangely *beautiful* about it.

The initial blow may have killed him for all I know (or care). He was standing and fishing, and then he was down and motionless. The *sound* was as satisfying as anything I have ever heard before or since. It was neither a *crack* nor a *thud*, but it was something sort of "in between" those two noises. I struggle with describing the sound any more clearly than that. A bird fled the scene in a panic, but I do not recall hearing much of anything else, apart from Ed crashing down along the river bank among some long weeds. For a moment, I stood near Ed's fallen body and waited to see if a second blow would be necessary. It was not. He did not move. I looked around. Nothing *else* was moving either, except for the water and the wind through the trees and weeds. Before I had gotten out of my car, I had put on some black work gloves with Kevlar on the knuckles. I also had a fixed-blade knife on my belt in case my "plan" (such as it was) had not gotten me the desired result. As it turns out, I did not need the knife. Ed was done.

The point of the term "dead weight" became clear to me as I struggled to get the body into the river. Ed was not a physically small man either. Pushing him into the water was difficult, but it was well worth the effort. There is nothing like the satisfaction of exerting significant physical effort to accomplish a goal successfully. Ed drifted a bit when I got him far enough out into the current. The river flowed by his carcass, and his motionless body got caught up in the stronger current soon enough. I watched his torso and legs make slow progress downstream for a bit, then I hurled his fishing pole out after him. That was all there was to it. I walked backward a few steps toward the bridge, and I watched Ed's body until I was satisfied that there was nothing more for me to do. Ed disappeared. Whether he went around a bend or sank is not entirely clear to me. It does not matter. Ed was gone. He disappeared. Ed and I never met. We never spoke. I just killed him. That is *all* I did with Ed. There was nothing else that I wanted to do with or to Ed. He *needed* killing and I killed him. That was my *entire* interest in this guy. I wanted to *end* him, and I did.

When I got home, I sat in silence for a long time. Trying to figure out how I felt about what I had done was, to say the least, an *odd* experience. It was certainly *novel*. To my surprise, I was not aware of feeling anything like guilt or panic. I had murdered a man, *legally* speaking, and there was *nothing* about what I had done that felt terrible to me. "Easy Ed" went down like a sack of potatoes, and I pushed his body into the river. The water carried him away. He disappeared from view. That was about all that had happened. There was nothing unique to the experience that felt "transformational" to me at the time. I had never killed anyone before. Ed was my first. I do not know if my initial foray into the "field" of killing people could have gone much more smoothly.

I had no idea what to expect next, and it was not clear to me whether I particularly *cared* what came next. Something had certainly changed, but I did not know what to make of it. Any attempt to describe or explain what went on in my mind would be awkward at best. I had turned myself into a *murderer*, as far as the *law* was concerned, and doing so did not trouble me at *all* at the time. Perhaps it troubles me on the odd occasion *these* days. I do *not* want to go to prison, after all. Then again, I cannot be certain that even the threat of prison *does* actually trouble me as much as, perhaps, it *should* (in some sense). The possibility of going to prison sometimes plays around the periphery of my consciousness, but the crime *itself* does not feel to me like much of a problem in and of *itself*. I *might* end up languishing in prison. That might be where *my* story is going to end.

Time will tell.

Describing the experience of becoming a murderer is not easy to communicate without lapsing into self-centered accounts of my own consciousness. I do not want to indulge in self-centeredness. Delving too deeply, for too long, into the inner workings of my mind is also uncomfortable for me. I prefer to describe my behavior, for the most part, and leave my thoughts in the background where, I think, they probably belong. It is one thing to murder people, but it is something else entirely to become a bore who blathers incessantly about how fascinating he finds his own stream of consciousness to be. A memoir inevitably involves a *bit* of that kind of thing. I *will* get back to my motives and purposes at some point, but it is a "muddy" and confusing area for me. That will become apparent to anyone who might read this.

Sometimes, it seems to me that there is all too much *psychologizing* in our culture. There is far too much attention paid to the reasons *why* miscreants do what they do. Is it not sufficient that an evil doer should be punished for his deeds? *Must* we obsess about causal antecedents, alleged childhood trauma, and all of the other topics through which psychologists are compelled to spend their careers sifting? Even when I was in school, my psychology courses bored me. I never developed the inclination to spend a lot of time wondering *why* other people did what they did. Observing their behavior is sufficient for me. One day, I may want to understand other people more thoroughly. Frankly, I doubt it.

Time will tell.

The Reason I Kill People

This is the "muddy" part. Living a "normal life" was something that I took for granted until I lost my entire family in a single devastating event. My life was a lot like any other "average" American life in the 21st Century. I watched television more frequently in the days before losing my family than I do now. These days, I only watch the news, and I do so only on fairly rare occasions.

My parents had both died from natural causes before my forty-fifth birthday. They were both smokers, and they both died of lung cancer. I suppose that counts as "natural causes" where smokers are concerned. Neither death was at all surprising. First came the emphysema, then the cancer, then the end. That is the way of things, and I was prepared to accept their deaths. Anyone could see it coming. Each of my parents saw it coming. They were no more surprised than me. The cancer diagnosis was met with something like a *shrug* from all of us. Sometimes, a shrug really is the best that anyone can do. That is probably worth remembering.

Presumably, I went through the grieving process in something like the standard fashion, or so I suppose in retrospect. How do people *usually* grieve? Nearly everyone expects to lose their parents at some point. I certainly did. A lifetime of smoking is not exactly conducive to longevity. *Some* smokers live a long time. Most do not. People who smoke, I assume, generally understand what they are doing to themselves. They mostly keep smoking anyway. Perhaps it is a form of slow-motion suicide. I cannot say for certain if my parents saw it this way or not. Their mental states do not fascinate any more than those of the strangers I encounter these days. The minds of others are none of my business. In any event, my parents did not seem to be desperate to live as long as possible. I can certainly understand that attitude.

Life goes on. As an only child, I inherited the entirety of their "estate" as lawyers call it, after the probate folks took their cut, of course. Though I had no desire to profit from their death, I *did* profit from it (though it may be crass to take note of this fact). When all was concluded, I found myself several hundred thousand dollars richer than I had been before, and I had been reasonably comfortable prior to their deaths. My former occupation is fairly lucrative. Why that should be so is something of a mystery to me, but I can say the same about a great deal of what goes on in the economic affairs that unfold all around me. I often find it difficult to understand why people are *paid* to do some of the things that they do for a living. It is as if many occupations are *invented* solely for the sake of keeping people occupied doing *something*. Perhaps that is for the best, after all. I do not know.

I have never been rich, by American standards, but I was not impoverished either. Forgive me if I do not mention many specifics about what I used to do for a living. First of all, it is hardly worth mentioning. Secondly, somebody might read this and become aware of connections that I prefer nobody should understand too clearly or too thoroughly. I do *not* want to go to prison.

Now that I no longer need to provide for a wife and children, and now that paying for college is an issue that will never arise for me, it turns out that I do not *need* to do much of anything to make money ever again, if I choose to ignore the business of "making a living" from now on. I am vaguely comfortable, in the *financial* sense, it seems. If it were up to me, I would trade every dollar I have just to get my family back, but that, of course, is simply *not* up to me, and it is, obviously, *not* an available option. All the money in the world cannot purchase new lives for the dead. Many people, I have no doubt, wish that it could be so. Ultimately, that kind of thing is not really "up to" any of us, and getting dead loved ones *back* is not an available option for anyone. Such is the way of things, I suppose. The dead *stay* dead no matter what the living might decide to do.

When my wife and children were destroyed in an automobile accident that left the car nearly unrecognizable *as* a car, and when it became clear that nobody other than my wife was really "at fault" for the accident, I simply had no idea what I was supposed to do with my life anymore. There was not even somebody to *sue* over the accident. There will be more to say about my wife's mistake later. That is an emotionally messy business for me.

After a respectable period of time, I took early retirement. It was actually a *very* early retirement, I suppose, but nobody at work really wanted me to be there anymore. I had become useless to my employer and my colleagues, even though nobody would have said so out loud. Everyone "understood" my decision, or so I was told. I could not have cared less about what anybody did or did not understand. That happens in *their* minds. None of my business. Shortly after negotiating my retirement package, I moved far from the place I had lived most of my adult life. There was no *life* worth living for me in *that* place anymore. Indeed, no specific place meant much of anything to me after I lost my family. We are told that "home is where the heart is," but "my heart" was nowhere in particular after the funeral. My family was in the ground. I did not need to be near those places in the ground. What do people hope to accomplish by visiting the gravesites of their loved ones? Is it all, ultimately, just something they do because they have been convinced that they are *supposed* to do it? The *people* they loved are *not* in those holes. There are dead *bodies* in there. Did they *love* the dead bodies? Those kinds of rituals and practices make no sense to me.

My initial goal was to "start over" in a new town where I knew nobody, nobody knew me or knew what had happened to my family, and I could, perhaps, hope to fashion some brand-new mode of existence for myself. The whole project might have been foolish and misguided. Does anyone ever *really* get to start over? The past does not just *disappear* from our lives. It colors and influences just about everything that we do and experience as we try to move forward. As it turns out, "forward" is not always such an easy course to chart. I had no idea which way was "forward" anymore. When a man realizes that he is lost, and that there really is "no direction home," anymore, to quote Bob Dylan, then moving "forward" looks a lot like going *nowhere* in particular. What is anybody supposed to do when *every* direction looks like it leads *away* from everything that ever mattered? Sometimes, all roads lead nowhere, or so it seemed to me at that time.

In any event, my experiences certainly had an impact on my choice to kill "Easy Ed" and on everything I have done since I sent Ed floating down that river. First and foremost, I no longer worried very much about what would happen to me in the immediate future, and I no longer had anyone else about whom I was obligated to be concerned. Filtering my decisions through concern for my family and their welfare had been keeping me in check, I guess, and it had been doing so in ways that I never would have considered if my wife had been a better driver. My wife *was*, after all, to blame for the accident. That is just *not* the way that I would like to remember her. She was a wonderful woman in just about every way I could have desired. Having *one* bad and dangerous habit while driving is hardly the worst sin anyone has ever committed. It is a *sin*, though, or so it seems to me. That bad habit changed everything for me, and I was not even in the car at the time. The accident changed everything that ever *really mattered* to *me*, in any event.

I was entirely on my own when Ed started shooting off his mouth in that bar. I was not merely *sitting* by myself. I was *alone* in the world, as far as I was concerned. In fact, I am *still* alone in the world, as I see it. These days, I am inclined to believe that being alone is probably the best way for me to be in the world as it now stands for me. Things are just easier that way. Having people to love would really complicate my life as I live it these days. I do *not* like the inconvenience of needless complications in my life. I prefer to keep things relatively simple. I am a simple man these days. My interests are fairly limited. That works for me, I suppose. Interpersonal connections have *not* worked out very well in my experience. Having a *family* did not work out very well at all.

None of the foregoing is, I am well aware, an excuse for committing murder (if my *kills* count as "murder" in the *moral* sense). Needing an "excuse" is not part of my list of concerns, though. I have simply decided that I will kill some of the people who really *need* to be killed. I have plenty of free time these days, after all. The world has *plenty* of terrible people in it. The ones I have killed will hardly be missed, if I am reading the circumstances correctly. If I am misreading circumstances, so be it. Let them be missed if that is the way that things need to be. Like anyone else, I am also quite imperfect when it comes to figuring out who wants what, or which persons are more or less likely to have an impact that is not so readily apparent. Human beings are mysterious creatures. They can stay that way for all I care.

If anyone wept for Ed, then those tears were probably for show. I will bet that Ed's wife was not terribly disappointed to be rid of him once and for all. His children will probably be better off without him, unless their mother chooses another husband cut from the same cloth as their father. Maybe I did that family some good. I am not, however, so delusional as to claim that benefiting Ed's family was my primary goal. I just wanted to kill that awful person for the *sake* of killing a thoroughly awful person. He *needed* killing, and I got rid of him. Any ancillary benefits are beside the point.

I am *not* a *good* man. Nobody should pretend to believe the contrary. I am not a "noble vigilante" roaming the countryside doing my best to protect the innocent. My life was ripped away from me, and I am no longer inclined to be civil and gentle toward evil people who need to be removed from the surface of the planet. I do *not* do what I do for the *sake* of helping others. I kill evil people because I *want* to kill evil people. There is not much more to it than *that*.

Unfortunately, most of the people who need killing are far beyond my reach. I am not a *trained* assassin. There is nothing like special forces experience in my background. Nobody in the CIA ever taught me how to use the "tools of the trade" for dispatching enemies of the state or for making an assassination look like an accident. I have lived most of my life as an extraordinarily ordinary guy. Hollywood does not make many movies about people like *me*. I am not sufficiently skilled to beat up a bar room full of bad guys. Those guys mostly exist *only* in the movies. If they exist in reality, then I suppose they are impressive specimens, but I am not endowed with those abilities. I know how to fight, but I am *neither* Batman nor The Equalizer. I inhabit the *real* world. That is, to my way of thinking, both a blessing and a curse.

The only advantage I may enjoy over some other murderers is that I am precisely the kind of guy that attracts very little attention when I walk into a room. The police never look twice in my direction. If I sit at a table next to a cop at a coffee shop, the cop pays me no mind whatsoever. I look very much like a middle-aged man with a job in some office somewhere. In fact, I actually *had* a job in some office somewhere. Although I am fairly large and powerful, I am not the kind of guy who goes to a lot of trouble to *look* large and powerful. For the most part, I tend to wear loose-fitting clothing, and I generally speak softly on the rare occasions that I speak at all. I suspect I look a bit like a middle-aged *farmer*. Who is intimidated by a middle-aged farmer? Those guys rarely cause any real trouble, right? It is good for me to look like a guy who rarely causes trouble. People who look like trouble-makers tend to attract a lot of attention. I prefer to attract *none*.

Most of the people with whom I once worked have probably forgotten that I exist. As it turns out, that makes my new life a little easier. If someone who has met me should read this account of my illegal actions, it is very likely that my name will *not* even occur to that person. Indeed, even the account of the accident that took my family from me is not terribly uncommon. At least one of my former co-workers experienced much the same thing. I sometimes wonder what *that* guy is up to these days. He has probably remarried by now. Good for him. He is "moving on" with his life, as they say. There is something admirable about that, I suppose.

As for me, the idea of starting a new family has never appealed to me at all. I had a family. It did *not* end well. Killing men like Ed, however, appeals to me a great deal. If that makes me a terrible person, then so be it. I still believe in God, for whatever that is worth, and I still believe that I will (probably) have to answer to Him when my time comes. I do not expect God to treat me gently. Then again, I cannot claim any greater insight into the will of the Almighty than anyone else. I will have more to say about *that* later.

If it turns out that there is *no* God, on the other hand, then it seems to me that anything goes as far as killing terrible people is concerned. Dostoyevsky was right about that, as far as I can tell. I cannot make any sense out of moral laws in the absence of an ultimate moral law *giver*. What I have done *is* murder in the *legal* sense, to be sure, but it does not follow that killing Ed and others of his ilk is necessarily *immoral*. Without God *nothing* is either morally good or evil, or so it seems to me. So, either God decides whether I am a murderer who deserves punishment, or some mere legal tribunal of other mortals like myself will judge my actions should I be caught one day. I can live with either eventuality until my time comes. For now, my new project continues until someone stops me.

Time will tell.

My goal has nothing to do with exacting any type of vengeance on the world that deprived me of my family. Nobody *owes* me *anything*. I committed a crime of opportunity against Ed, and I have never yet regretted that choice. Ed was not, however, the *last* man I decided to destroy. There are *plenty* of terrible people in the world. Perhaps we will all pay the price for this, as did (allegedly) the people of Noah's day. Does anyone really believe that people today are morally *superior* to those who perished in the great deluge? God promised not to kill us all with a *flood* again. He did not promise that He would not do us all in via some other method, did He? We might just push our Creator (if we *have* a Creator) too far one more time, and He may grow tired of us once again. Given everything that the human race insists upon getting up to, it is hard to blame God for being disappointed with us. Then again, if He exists, then He, presumably, *knew* what we were going to do. Perhaps there is some overarching plan, and maybe I will understand it at some point. Then again, maybe I will live, die, cease to exist, and remain as ignorant as I am today. I can easily imagine living another thousand years without ever understanding any more about the human condition than I understand right now. Thankfully, I will *not* live another thousand years. For all I know, I will not live to see very many more days at all.

Time will tell.

I Read Scripture

I have read both the *Bible* and the *Quran*. They are probably the two most fascinating documents I have ever encountered. They are popular books for *good* reason. There is an awful lot of *killing* in each of those texts, by the way. Not *all* of it appears to be condemned by the Creator, as far as I can tell, at any rate. In fact, my reading indicates that the Lord *requires* the death penalty for a *host* of different crimes and sins. Read *Leviticus*. Read the list of crimes for which God demands the *life* of the perpetrators.

According to the *Genesis* account about Noah and the flood, God saw fit to destroy the entire human race, with the exception of the few people on the ark, and my reading indicates to me that He killed off nearly all of humanity because they *deserved* it. If *everybody* can deserve to die, or *nearly* everybody, then it seems to follow as a matter of simple logic and mathematics that *some* people can deserve to die, does it not? Granted, I am not in the same position as the Almighty to render such judgment, but I am not a *snail* either. We humans are endowed, mostly, with the faculty of *reason*. We can be held *morally* accountable for our behavior. We can hold *others* morally accountable. I guess that *could* eventually prove to be *my* undoing.

Time will tell.

Read the rest of the *Bible* for plenty of other examples of God demanding that the blood of those who commit various sins must be shed by the hand of *man*. God demands that *we*, *not* He, must take care of imposing justice for certain types of misdeeds, and the enactment of justice He demands *execution* for the deeds that are most heinous and hateful to Him. At what point did these injunctions expire? At what point did the collective will of humanity supplant the Commandments of our Creator? I never got the memo. There are, according to scripture, people that we are *supposed* to kill, or so it seems to me. Consider what God said to Noah just after the flood waters had receded:

Whoever sheds the blood of man,
by man his blood will be shed;
for in His own image
God has made mankind.

So, it looks to me like God has instructed *man* to shed the blood of those people who insist upon misbehaving by shedding the blood of other men. Ed shed human blood. He may not have killed anyone, as far as I know, but did God *not* intend for guys like Ed to be killed by men like me? I must request *evidence* that God wants people like Ed to keep living and torturing their families. What kind of God would want those guys to keep living? Did I *murder* Ed? According to man's law, I did. Am I not, however, *also* a man, and do I not, also, have the capacity to render judgment about what Ed deserves? If God wants us to kill *anyone*, then it is difficult for me to believe that Ed does *not* qualify as the kind of human being that God wants us to clear from His world. Maybe that is just a rationalization on my part. So be it. Ed is dead. The world *must* be a slightly better place now that Ed is no longer a living part of it, right? Again, I do not claim that making the world a better place is my *reason* for doing away with Ed or the others. I kill people because I think they *need* killing. *Justice* is not up to me.

The Quran is also a fairly blunt document where transgression and punishment are concerned. It is well worth reading. Too many people in the West refuse to give Islamic scripture a chance, as far as I am concerned. One often-misapplied verse of the *Quran* tells us:

Kill them wherever you come upon them and drive them out of the places from which they have driven you out. For persecution is far worse than *killing*.

From this, I gather that the Muslim holy book holds the "persecutor" to be an even more evil agent than the man who kills the persecutor. Well, if Ed was not guilty of *persecuting* his wife and children, then the drinks are on me. What *is* beating, torture, and oppression by physical force if it is *not* persecution. To be clear, however, I did not kill Ed and the others because I believed that I was doing "God's work" or anything enjoined upon me by some holy book or other. My motivation does *not* derive from an overarching concern to please my Creator or anyone else. I am *not* waging *jihad*. Perpetrating evil in God's name, we are told in the Ten Commandments, is the one sin that God will *not* forgive, or such is my interpretation, in any event. I do not kill in God's name or at His behest. Nobody should blame religion, or God, or scripture, or anyone or anything other than *me*, when it comes to the men that I have killed. I, and I *alone*, am responsible for all of the evil that I have done. Which parts of my deeds are, indeed, evil? Frankly, I cannot say with anything approaching certainty. Perhaps I will eventually come to understand the nature of good and evil better than I do today.

Time will tell.

No, I do not claim to be an "avenging angel" working on God's behalf. The thought of God's Commands did *not* cross my mind when I took that tire thumper to Ed's skull. I did not push his motionless body into the river as an act of divine retribution. I killed Ed because I *wanted* to kill him, and because I regarded him as something like a rabid dog masquerading as a man. I put him down like a sick animal. My conscience does not trouble me about what I did to Ed, as far as I am aware, at any rate (who can speak for the subconscious and unconscious mind?). Perhaps this is a massive character flaw on my part. I can accept that. If I am a *murderer* for killing Ed, then I will live with that. Ed, however, will stay *dead*. If I face punishment for what I have done, then I will do so like the kind of man of integrity that Ed was *not*. I will never *deny* killing that rabid dog. There is no *good* reason to claim that I did *not* put him down like a sick animal. I did it, officer. I am guilty. The chips will fall where they may. No matter what happens to me, Ed will still be dead. That is just fine as far as I am concerned. This is how things seem to me *today*.

Time will tell.

Verses of scripture other than those aforementioned are, not surprisingly, far less comforting to me when I consider what I have done and what I *failed* to do. There is something to be found in both the *Bible* and the *Quran* for just about any *mood* in which one might find oneself, after all.

If the "peacemakers" are "blessed," then what the hell should we conclude about those, like myself, who *refuse* to make peace? Passages that extol the virtue of *forgiveness* do not comport very well with bashing in the skulls of people I *decline* to forgive, do they? Believing in God is something of a dicey proposition for killers who slay evil doers. We do not get to cherry pick the text, if we want to be *honest* with ourselves. *Nobody* gets to do *that* with a clear conscience, I suspect. Of course, people still *do* it all the time.

The *Quran* has a few things to say about killing without *legal* justification. Here is just *one* example:

> *Do not take a human life—made sacred by Allah—except with legal right. If anyone is killed unjustly, We have given their heirs the authority, but do not let them exceed limits in retaliation, for they are already supported by law.*

Well, I do not think any of man's laws "supported" what I did to Ed, nor does any law "support" the other kills I mention in this memoir. So, converting to Islam would probably not "save my soul," given what I have done. Then again, I do not claim to *know* what saves souls.

Jewish scripture, Christian scripture, and Islamic scripture are all ambiguous at best regarding the kinds of things I have done since I lost my entire family. Well, they are ambiguous as far as I am able to tell, at any rate. Of course, I do not read Hebrew, Greek, Latin, or Arabic. I am sure that *something* is lost in translation. I work with what I have. My understanding is at least as limited as is anyone else's understanding where scripture is concerned. None of us gets to understand the mind of God, as far as I know. In any event, that kind of thing is certainly beyond *me*.

Buddhism and Hinduism do not seem to be "helpful" for a guy who wants to find some type of excuse for killing people either. Whether I *need* an excuse, whether I should *want* to be excused, and whether I have committed sins that will cost me an eternity of punishment are questions that sometimes scare the *hell* out of me. Ed was my *first* kill. He was *not* my last. How does a *serial* killer (if I *qualify* as one) find solace in words that allegedly come from the Creator of all human life? Well, who the hell said that serial killers should find *solace* anywhere? I do *not* search for solace *anywhere*. I seek *understanding,* but I do not expect that I will achieve greater understanding to bring me peace of mind, or to reward me with serenity. I expect to wander somewhat uneasily through the rest of my life.

Time will tell.

I will continue to try and figure out the proper moral assessment of the things that I have done. If anyone ever reads these pages, then perhaps other people will offer their judgment about the deeds they find described here. If that happens, then I will surely be condemned by some of those who offer comment.

There is no particular reason to *dispute* any condemnation that may one day be hurled in my direction. Most killers are, it is fairly safe to say, people who *deserved* to be condemned and punished. There may be a great deal of both condemnation and punishment in my future. More suffering may be visited upon me at the hands of other persons, and God, if He exists, will serve as the final arbiter of my actions. What punishment might God apply to a wretch like me?

Time will tell.

Consider the very *first* murder mentioned in *Genesis*. God informs Cain that his brother Abel's blood "cries out" from the soil. Cain is then punished with a curse directly imposed upon him by his Creator. He is to be a "restless wanderer" for the rest of his days. God, according to *Genesis*, not to mention *Exodus*, *Leviticus*, and many other books of scripture, does *not like* murder or murderers. The crime is listed in the *Ten Commandments* for good reason. My crimes are, without question, murders as far as the *laws of the land* are concerned. My crimes may also qualify as *murders* as far as *God* is concerned. I do not claim to be confident of the contrary. Murder, as I understand it, is the act of killing innocent people or killing in a morally unjustifiable fashion. I do not know, nor do I even *claim*, that my kills have been morally justified. Even if they *are* justifiable, that is *not* my motive for killing the men that I have killed. I neither claim nor *seek* any moral justification for what I have done. I wanted to kill terrible people, and I have done so. That is all. I have "shed the blood" of men who were (allegedly) made in God's image. There may be no salvation for me.

Time will tell.

When "push comes to shove," (and when has push ever *not* come to shove?), I am mystified by morality. If there *are* moral laws, then those laws *can* be broken. Laws of physics *cannot* be broken. Laws of mathematics *cannot* be broken. The only other laws that *can* be broken are *civil* laws. Those are nothing

more than human *constructs*. If moral laws, like civil laws, are
nothing more than human constructs, then *where* am I supposed
to find the *morality* in them? Why would it be immoral to violate
commands that are *invented* by other human beings who are
just as flawed as I am? Am I *really* supposed to be bound and
compelled to behave as some legislature (filled with *politicians!*)
demands that I behave? Either God imposes the moral laws, or
there are *no such things* as moral laws at all. I decline to submit
to the will of anyone other than God. If there is no God, then
I decline to submit to *anyone's* will. A collective is not wiser
than an individual merely because it *is* a collective. There are,
to be sure, *practical* reasons to obey laws, or to avoid being
caught breaking laws, but there is nothing beyond practical
concerns where mere *civil* laws are concerned. It is *not* immoral
to refuse to obey the governing bodies of one's nation. Slavery
was perfectly legal throughout most of human history in nearly
every nation on the face of the planet. Slaves did not, for *legal*
reasons, commit *immoral* acts when they escaped from their
owners. Maybe there *could* be a society that bases legislation
only on its understanding of scripture and on its conception
of God's laws. Maybe there could be a viable and legitimate
theocracy somewhere on this planet. There have been several
illegitimate ones, or so it seems to me. Legislation that is based
solely on scripture has never happened yet, but it *could*. Would
a nation governed by God's laws be a better society than those
that are governed by men? Perhaps the world will learn the
answer to this question at some point or other.

Time will tell.

My *favorite* book from all of the scripture I have ever read
is the *Book of Job*. The title character of that book lost *his* entire
family much as I lost mine. He was stripped of everything
that really mattered to him in the world that he inhabited. Job
managed to maintain his faith in God, for the most part, but
his suffering drove him to insist upon an *explanation* from the

Almighty. Job demanded to know what he had done to deserve the fates visited upon him. So, God appeared to Job in the form of a whirlwind. Not surprisingly, God did *not* feel obligated to explain anything to the talking primate He had created. Indeed, God seemed to be *angered* by the demand. He asked Job, "Where were you," and He presented a litany of the things that He had created, as well as the things that *only* God could ever know or understand. God reprimanded Job for his complaint. Job repented of his ingratitude, and admitted that he spoke without knowledge or understanding. There is a crucial lesson in that.

Does the Lord owe a *justification* of his plans to a creature that exists only because God created him, and also created an entire world for him to inhabit? Is God's creation not *good* enough for Job? Does Job pretend to know what *must* be, and what must *not* be, if God's overarching plans and designs are to be brought to fruition? The temerity of Job's demand is more than God is willing to tolerate from a creation of His devising. The world is the way that it is because the Author of all creation has made it so. That is all that any of us can know about why the world is the way that it is. That will have to be sufficient for *all* of us.

The created creature can *never* understand why the world must be as it is. What is man, that God should pay him any heed at all, to paraphrase another bit of scripture. The *Psalms* remind us that we are not to be so ungrateful as to complain about the role we are assigned in the *Grand and Powerful Play* of God's authorship. Job's suffering caused him to forget that God never *had* to create him at all. When Job lost his family, his possessions, and his health, it all felt like an *injustice* to him. What could Job possibly *know*, however, about what is or is not *just*? How could a mere talking primate know what is or is not necessary? Where *was* Job, after all, when God "laid the firmament," created the stars, or separated the light from the darkness? Job was *nowhere.* God had not yet *created* him.

If each of us exists *only* because God saw fit to take the trouble to create each of us and, thereby, give us an opportunity to live a unique and unrepeatable human life, then who among us should *dare* to complain about *anything* that this world has to offer? Sometimes, I imagine God challenging *me* in the way that he challenged Job. Indeed, I strongly suspect that this is a central purpose of that particular book of the *Bible*. Job is an allegory for the human condition at large, I think. Sometimes, I try to comfort myself by reference to my family's demise as a necessary part of God's plan that I can never understand any better than Job could possibly hope to understand the events *he* experienced. Sometimes I think that I *am* Job. The Lord *gave* me a family, and the Lord *took* that family away. Do I *dare* complain about my lot in this life? Well, I have, on occasion, *dared* to begrudge God *this* element of his plan. I *also* want an explanation. Unlike Job, God has not bothered to appear to me in a whirlwind. That story has already been told, after all. How many times must God present us with a lesson before we see fit to take the trouble to *learn* the lesson in question? Perhaps I do not warrant even a "dressing down" as did Job. Nobody bothered to include a book about *me* in scripture, after all. What am I that the Lord should take any notice of me or be mindful of anything about me? That is a good question, or so it seems to me.

If there *is* a God, and I do not pretend to *know* that there is, then I suppose that God has the right to do with me, and to do with everyone and everything else He has created, whatever He sees *fit* to do with the whole thing. Other people have suffered *far* worse fates than I have endured, have they not? Where do I get off complaining about *any* facet of a world that I do not understand and that I clearly could not have created? I am painfully aware that there is something *shameful* about whining and carping my way through the rest of my life. Even if God does *not* exist, then I am still here by virtue of something like a miraculous series of *accidents* within the natural world. The world does not *need* me in it. The world does not *need* my family in it. Of *that*, I am very certain. After all, my family is *gone* (in some sense), and the world is still *here*. I am still here as well. The *Book of Job*, by *my* reading of it at any rate, informs us that none of us can ever hope to understand the fundamental nature of the world, and none of us is owed any *explanation* of *anything* at all. *Here* is the world. *Here* am I. Nature is *not* of *my* making. I have been given an opportunity to live a human life, and I have the capacity to reason, to experience psychological and emotional complexity that is available, as far as I can tell, to *no* other species of life on this planet. Is all of *that* "not good enough" for me? Am I *entitled* to have a happy, healthy family, and to escape the suffering that attends *losing* my family? Am I *entitled* to *anything*? Ultimately, I am *not*. How could I be *entitled* to anything? Indeed, I am not even *entitled* to my next *breath*. I am nothing more than another talking primate roaming the surface of a planet in an unimaginably vast universe. I am *nothing*. Perhaps I can, eventually, make peace with my lot in this life. Perhaps I will *never* be at ease in this world.

Time will tell.

My Second Kill

It is not terribly difficult to find men who have raped children. An internet search will reveal all the information that one can stomach. They get released from prison but still, for reasons I do not understand, are permitted to live among other people, some of whom *are* children. If the death penalty is applied to *anyone* in our society, then there is simply *no* good reason not to execute these filthy predators, or so I would argue. I do *not* care what the Supreme Court says about the matter. If murderers can be executed, then men who murder the souls of little children, and who violate their tiny bodies for sexual gratification, are at least as deserving of the same punishment. In prisons all over the nation, convicted murderers will *not* allow child molesters to live among them. Even *murderers* are disgusted by these filthy *things* masquerading as people, and they do not hesitate to register their disgust by carrying out executions of their own. I agree with the murderers here. This is not partisanship, either. Even before I became a murderer myself, I always thought that the world would be a better place if we killed every child rapist on the planet. They should *all* dangle from the end of a short rope. I will not shed a tear for *any* of them. Does *anyone*?

In fact, I got rid of one not too long after dispatching Ed to Hell or to nothingness. As it turns out, the local library was a very useful instrument for finding the guy who followed Ed out of this life by my hand. This filthy *creature* had been convicted of raping *several* children, to say nothing of the children he defiled without being caught for doing so. Again, I do not imagine that anyone wept for him after he disappeared. If his parents are still alive, I am willing to bet that even *they* do not miss him. In any event, he is gone now. He will never lay his filthy claws on a child ever again. Like Ed, he is *done*. I sent him on his way.

My conscience does not trouble me in the *slightest* over what I did to him. I think I am actually proud of it. *Pride*, of course, is one of the seven deadly sins. We would all do well to remember that, I think.

Libraries typically have computers available for public use. That is a valuable service for people who do not want certain search histories listed on their computers at home. A search for convicted sex offenders might cause trouble for me if my home computer is ever seized by the authorities. *My* computer is *clean*. The library's computers are not likely to become my problem. The library in question is *nowhere* near my home. Maybe some diligent law enforcement official could make the connection with sufficient effort, but how hard are the police going to work to figure out who killed the guy that raped all of those little kids? I suspect they have more pressing concerns. They are not likely to come looking for me. If that particular murder is ever discovered, and to date I have seen no evidence that anyone knows what happened, I suspect the cops will not exert much effort to find me.

Time will tell.

Travis was a registered sex offender, and that is how I found out where he lived and (*some* of) what he had done. I will never understand a legal system that regards these criminals as sufficiently dangerous that they must be on a sex offender registry, but *not* sufficiently dangerous that they ought to stay in prison for the rest of their miserable lives. If the law will not allow for their execution, then, for God's sake, at least keep these *things* locked up for the rest of their days, right? Well, nobody cares what I think about anything. I cannot blame the various nobodies for not much caring what I have to say about *anything*. Who the hell am I, after all? So, I solved the problem of Travis myself. *Somebody* had to do it, I suppose. In any event, somebody *did* do it. In that sense, and *only* in that sense, I *am* somebody.

It took significantly more planning to rid the world of Travis than was necessary to put Ed out of everybody's misery. Travis was not a fisherman. That was inconvenient for me. I dislike being inconvenienced. Breaking into Travis' house was not an appealing option. Never follow a predator into his lair if doing so can be avoided while still accomplishing the goal, I always say. Well, I do not *always* say that, I guess. He also lived more than an hour away from where I lived at the time. I no longer live in that place. Travis no longer lives *anywhere*. It is best to put distance between myself and the places where I have killed people. As for the "distance" between the dead and the living they leave behind, I do not feel qualified to say much. Travis is far enough from his victims and from other children for *my* liking. Travis will never touch another child anywhere on this planet. That is just fine as far as I am concerned.

This might be surprising, but it turns out that Travis had something of a "substance abuse" problem. This became apparent to me from observing Travis intermittently over a period of a few weeks. I had to drive a fair distance on these reconnaissance missions, but I do not really mind commuting to work if it is for a limited time. There is a park not too far from the apartment where Travis lived. I noticed children playing in that park on more than one occasion. So, Travis, it seems, bought his drugs just outside of a park frequented by neighborhood kids. That was all I needed to see. Actually, I did not *need* to see even that much, but witnessing him standing near children steeled my resolve to get rid of this guy. Travis would never touch one of those children, if I had anything to say about it. I did. He did *not* touch those children or, at the very least, he will never do so again.

Many of us are creatures of habit. We have our typical patterns and rhythms. I like to drink two cups of coffee right after I wake up. It aids the gut motility necessary to clear my bowels for a day without having to worry about too many bathroom breaks.

That comes in handy. Nothing disrupts a stakeout quite like a bowel movement. It is difficult to observe miscreants from a bathroom stall (usually). That kind of thing is just inconvenient. I do not like to be inconvenienced.

Travis liked to buy his drugs at the playground just after dark. Perhaps he would have been better off with coffee at home. We never had a chance to discuss the matter. I do not recall seeing Travis go to a local bar or saloon. Maybe people in his town knew what he was and did not want him drinking near them. I do not know. I do not care. All I really needed to know was that Travis walked from his apartment to the park around the same time of day, on *most* days anyway, and that he returned home by the same route he took to the park. His route took him through an alley about half way between his apartment and the park. Travis *died* in that alley.

There was a large and conveniently located dumpster in the passageway between buildings that Travis used as a shortcut. It was just outside the backdoor of a restaurant. Travis was *not* a large man. He was short and thin. He probably weighed about 125 pounds. From my brief experience with Travis, I suspect he never studied any jiu-jitsu. At any rate, he did not seem to know the standard counters for the rear naked choke. In professional wrestling, which I watched as a kid, they called this maneuver the "sleeper hold," but the Brazilian practitioners had elevated the rear naked choke to something of an art form. Unlike Travis, I *have* studied a fair bit of jiu-jitsu. The rear naked choke is my go-to submission. I learned to wrap it up quickly, and to apply it in a manner that makes shouting or crying out very difficult. It is best to "take the back" and to remain standing if the opponent is sufficiently shorter and smaller. In the dojo, a man caught in a choke he cannot escape generally "taps out" to indicate that he prefers not to be rendered unconscious. Competitors in the dojo are generally about the same size. This is an attempt to make the competition *fair*.

There are no "weight classes" in alleys. There are also no rules or referees. Travis could have used a ref's intervention. As it happens, there was nobody there to pull me off of him. Travis had no idea that anyone else was in that alley until it was too late for him to respond effectively. When I stepped out from behind the dumpster, grabbed him, and wrapped up the choke, he managed to croak, "Ah," but I increased the pressure around his throat and carotid arteries very rapidly to stifle his voice, and cut off the oxygen to his brain. The rear naked choke is a *blood* choke. The goal is to deprive the brain of oxygen. It *works*.

He was unconscious in about eight seconds by my estimation. That was how long it took for him to stop kicking my shins and flailing his arms. He should have tried to get ahold of my hands and break "the lock" on the choke. Travis either did not know how to do this, or he panicked and malfunctioned under duress. It makes no difference to me either way. He was probably *dead* in under thirty seconds. The brain cannot continue to function for very long without sufficient oxygen. His brain was deprived of oxygen for a *very* long time. I held the choke until my arms felt like they were on fire. It is unwise to take chances in such cases. His feet never touched the ground again after I hoisted him high enough so that my chin was touching his ear. I am *not* a physically small man. I am much taller than Travis. It was not a "fair fight" at all. I can live with that. Travis died dangling. I can live with *that* as well. Travis, it turns out, could *not*.

After I gently and quietly lowered his body into the large dumpster, I carefully covered Travis' body with several layers of trash bags and restaurant refuse. There was also a discarded rug in the dumpster, and that came in handy for hiding the corpse. I moved food, napkins, rags, and all sorts of other detritus on top of his body. It seemed fitting to me that Travis should end up in the trash. Anyone opening that dumpster, even in broad daylight, would probably never have seen Travis, unless there was some reason to climb inside and root around searching for something that some customer had lost. Even if someone *had* found his body, I was long gone and never returned to the scene of the crime. It is baffling to me that some criminals actually *do* that. It is just such a pathetic cliché. What kind of idiot "returns to the scene of the crime" without necessity? I have never returned to the town where Travis died. There is nothing there for me now. I came, I saw, I choked Travis to death, and I disposed of the body as best I was able given the conditions. Why would I return to that place? I had *nothing* else to do with the town in question. I will never go back there. My work in that place is done.

If anyone discovered Travis' body, I never heard or read about it. Like Ed, he just kind of disappeared from the face of the planet as far as anyone seemed to know or care. Evidently, the "manhunt" for a convicted child molester is a limited endeavor. My guess is that *nobody* ever looked for that little prick. If anybody *did* search for him, then it was probably some drug dealer to whom he owed money, and that drug dealer would probably have killed him anyway. That is just the way it goes sometimes, I suppose. Some people just are not meant to last very long living among the rest of us. Men who *rape* children are, I suspect, right at the very top of the list of people who are not fit company for "polite society" among families and children, or even among drug dealers and murderers. Then again, it might just be that those disgusting *things* are everywhere. I have really begun to wonder about how many child rapists there may be. I do not know. There are a distressing number of reports of their crimes in the news, are there not? What kind of a pandemic of degeneracy is our culture facing these days? Has it *always* been this way? Have there always been hordes of child molesters roaming the quiet countryside and victimizing the most innocent among us? If so, then ours has always been a *depraved* species. In any event, there are fewer child molesters in *that* particular town than there were before I got my hands on Travis. I subtracted one from their number. Maybe someone will discover Travis' skeleton in a landfill somewhere. Maybe nobody will ever bother to look wherever he ended up.

Time will tell.

Doubts Arise

After I deposited Travis in the dumpster, I went home by a circuitous route. Where else was I supposed to go? Once home, I found myself wondering if Travis had, perhaps, become a sex predator because *he* had been victimized by some other rabid dog as a child. Many of these people become child molesters as a result of their own childhood trauma and victimization, or so I have read. Did Travis *deserve* to die, if he became what he was because of what had been done *to* him?

Ultimately, I decided, it really makes no difference to me. If I find a rabid dog, my first concern is not *how* the animal contracted rabies. It is too late to do much about *that* once the virus has been transmitted and the symptoms become apparent. The animal cannot be saved. The only humane thing to do with a beast exhibiting the symptoms of rabies is to put it down in short order. It cannot be cured. It cannot be salvaged. It is, as they used to say, "no good to itself no more," and somebody has to take care of it in the only manner that can solve the problem of the rabid animal. It *needs* killing. There is no other viable solution to the problem. My assessment of Travis was something along the same lines of the general assessment of a rabid dog. He *needed* killing.

Who am I, however, to serve as judge, jury, and executioner? I have no answer to that question, and I do not know that I will *ever* have one. That works just fine for me. How "high" is the bar for being qualified to render that kind of judgment about another human being (even one who is essentially the moral equivalent of a rabid dog)? The legal system did not see fit to execute Travis the child rapist. What entitles *me* to do what the legal system declined to do? Well, *nothing*. Indeed, I do not even *claim* to be "entitled" to kill people. All I know is that I *have* done it. I wanted Ed and Travis to die, and they are both dead now because I decided that I wanted it that way. Do I have the "moral authority" to kill people? Am I qualified to decide how to apply God's laws? Hey, I do not even know for sure that God exists! As far as Ed and Travis are concerned, I do not really care whether God sanctions my actions or not. If I were an atheist, then I *still* would have killed those two lumps of human debris. If there *is* a God, then it is quite likely that God will punish me for what I have done, I suppose. *That* is not up to me. Ultimately, very little is up to me. One way or another, I suspect we all end up paying what we owe. What I "owe" for putting an end to a child molester and a wife-beater is not entirely clear to me. Those two were morally terrible people, as far as I can tell, in any event. Something *had* to be done about them. I did what *needed* to be done. That is my judgment of the matter. I did what I *wanted* to do to those two people who tortured the innocent.

This is not because I believe that this "vale of tears" is an inherently *just* or fair place. I was *not* enacting *justice*. I have lived long enough to see far too many people "get away" with being utterly terrible, at least as far as their lives on this planet might be concerned. If God's justice is inescapable, then everyone will have to face the music. If there is *no* God, then the drinks are on me, as I often say. Perhaps the human condition is meaningless and nothing more than the result of a string of accidents culminating in conscious, reasoning creatures who tend to struggle to convince themselves that there is *some* *purpose* to the whole thing. It might just be that we all get to learn the truth of our place in this world after we die. A lot of people certainly seem to cleave to the belief that we ultimately get something like *answers* to the questions that sometimes keep us up at night. Maybe that intuition, or that desperate *hope*, will prove to be based in something that the Creator has woven into the fundamental fabric of humanity. Maybe our conscience comes from our Creator. It might just be that the human conscience is a "spark of the divine" by reference to which we are supposed to guide and govern our conduct. Then again, many of us might be just fooling ourselves. If the atheists are right, then any "purpose" we encounter is probably nothing more than another human construct, and I am not impressed with the moral "inventions" of the human race. Humans invent all kinds of things without which we would all probably be better off, in *some* sense. At the moment, I do not have *any* answers about our moral duties. Perhaps there are *no* answers to be had. Maybe I will figure some of this out before my life is over.

Time will tell.

I readily confess to doubts about the actions I have taken. These doubts pale in comparison to the satisfaction I have derived from killing the people I have killed. Perhaps "satisfaction" is not the optimal word for what I have experienced. I *needed* to kill the people that I have killed. I can offer very little more than *that* by way of explanation. A more talented writer could probably come up with something more apt. I am *not* a more talented writer. Indeed, I am not a writer by training at all. Just writing this stuff down does not make me a *writer*, does it? I also swim sometimes, but I would not describe myself as a "swimmer." Michael Phelps is a swimmer. I am not a Michael Phelps. I have never competed in the Olympics. We cannot all have real talent in *every* area, can we? My abilities are very limited. I am certainly nobody special. There will be no Olympic gold for me. So be it.

Ed and Travis were no more special than me, I suppose. I hope that they were *worse* people than I am. Of course, to the best of my knowledge, neither of them ever *murdered* anybody. Is the guy who kills people like Ed and Travis a morally worse human being than a wife-beater or a child rapist? I hope not. Beyond hoping, there is not a great deal I can do about our comparative decency. Most people are something of a "mixed bag" where moral decency is concerned, as far as I can tell. It is possible that I will learn the ultimate truth of this matter before I die, or after I am gone from this place.

Time will tell.

The School Bully

One of the memories that re-emerged after I lost my family concerned a school bully that I had to deal with in the sixth or seventh grade. Until recently, this had been a fairly distant and vague memory for me. Now, it seems as if it happened just last week. The whole thing is quite vivid for me these days. I do not know why that should be so. Nonetheless, it *is* so.

Chris was a real jerk as a kid. What he is like these days, if he is still alive, I have absolutely *no* idea. He might be a sweet guy these days. For all I know he is a "pillar of his community" as the expression has it. Sometimes, really lousy children grow up to be wonderful people. For all I know (or care), Chris grew up to be a very different man than anything about him might have indicated when he was just a lousy kid. I used to be a kid, after all. At the time, I did not kill people. I *almost* killed Chris, though. For a moment, I feared that I had done so, and that I would pay for it in the usual fashion. A visit from the police would not have surprised me at all. I have not had to pay for it just yet.

Time will tell.

At the time in question, I was *small* for my age. A few years later, I hit a growth spurt, and I doubt someone like Chris would have tried to bully me after that. Bullies, for the most part, really are *cowards* at heart. They do not want a *fair* fight against someone who has a real chance against them, but they *love* to torture smaller, weaker kids. I dislike bullies. Chris saw me as a good target when I was still one of the smaller kids in class. As they say, however, "it ain't the size of the dog in the fight," and I was a *mean* little doggy even then. Chris found out the hard way. I hope he learned a lesson. Maybe he did, or maybe he is just as bad as ever. He might be dead by now. That kind of thing is not really up to *me*, is it?

For several weeks, Chris had been making comments and giving me the "mad dog" look every chance he got. This was a mistake on his part. It is never a good idea to alert the "prey" that an attack is probably forthcoming. It gives the prospective target of one's attack an opportunity to either flee, or to prepare to fight. I never was much for fleeing. Instead, I simply started carrying a weapon in the front pocket of my pants. The weapon I used on Chris, and that I still have today, is called a "kubotan," though I did not know that at the time. It is designed to be slightly longer than a human hand, and one end of it, the striking end, is tapered to a rounded point. There are also two prongs that fit between the middle knuckles of the hand to prevent slippage upon impact. It is a force multiplier, and when delivering a "hammer fist" strike (a term I learned *long* after I used it on Chris), it focuses the damage on the part of the body struck by the rounded point. Used with sufficient force, it will break a bone or crush a muscle. This thing can inflict significant damage when used properly. Chris learned this the hard way. He *deserved* it, as far as I am concerned.

I knew where Chris lived. Our town was not very large. Over a few days, I followed Chris part of the way home, but was careful that he was not aware I was following at a distance. Evidently, I have something of a natural talent for that kind of thing. The day that Chris told me during lunch that he was going to "beat my ass," I followed him home for the final time. Chris did not make it home under his own power that day. Chris did not "beat my ass" as he had promised.

On this occasion, I had no interest in anything like a *fair* fight against the school bully. There is no obligation to be fair with someone like Chris. I just wanted to convince him that he should look elsewhere for a victim. I think I did that pretty successfully. In any case, Chris never bothered me again, and I have yet to pay any price for what I did to him.

Time will tell.

At an opportune moment, after Chris had turned off of the road on which our school was located, and he had headed down a side street toward his house, I did a quick check for potential witnesses and, seeing none, I rushed up behind Chris and slammed the point of my kubotan into the back of his neck as powerfully as I could. He went down in a heap and let out a cry like scalded dog. Quickly, I dropped one knee on his back, grabbed a handful of his hair, and wrenched his head back as far as I could pull it. Before he could speak a word, I put the rounded point of the kubotan to his right eyeball, held it hard against his lower eyelid. I said, "If you *ever* touch me, if you ever run your mouth at me, and if you ever so much as look at me the wrong way again, I will *kill* you." My hope was to make it clear that this was not a mere figure of speech. He said, "Hey," or something like that, and I quickly shifted my weight and struck him in the throat with the kubotan. I felt it sink into that vulnerable area, and I kept it pressed as deeply and as firmly as I could manage. Chris began to breathe heavily and whine. I yanked even harder on his hair and growled, "Shut up! Make another sound, and this thing goes through the back of your neck!" Chris went silent. I pressed the kubotan even harder into his throat to make my point clear to him. Chris stopped struggling. He looked absolutely terrified. That did *not* bother me.

I looked around, and a few kids were passing at a distance down the street from which Chris and I had turned. Nobody seemed to notice us in a heap on the sidewalk. Looking back down at Chris' terrified face, I said, "I *will* kill you. I will never warn you again. You had *better* understand me." Chris was frozen in place, and his mouth was open as if to scream, but he made no sound. I shifted my weight again, quickly raised the kubotan and then slammed it into the side of his head twice. That was all for Chris. He was unconscious. He went limp and his head fell against the sidewalk when I released my grip on his hair. Looking around one more time, I stood up, kicked Chris in the groin as hard as I could, and waited for a response. There was none. Chris was, luckily, still breathing. I had not killed him. Satisfied that I had made my point, I turned and walked back to my house. Chris did not come to school for the rest of the week.

I fully expected someone from the school or some other kind of authority to show up at my door. Chris knew where I lived, after all. We lived in, as I indicated, a fairly small town at the time. To my surprise, *nothing* happened. The consequences I awaited never materialized.

Time will tell.

Chris came back to school the next week. His demeanor had changed significantly. He never approached me again, and never spoke another word to me. A rumor circulated that Chris had badly injured himself in a bicycle accident. There are, after all, *many* ways to injure oneself. Kids wreck their bikes all the time, right? Beyond my heightened concerned for a few weeks, there were no other consequences, or none that came to my attention. As far as I could tell, I had gotten away with the assault, and nobody other than Chris and me knew what had happened. I have no idea where Chris is today. I do not care. He is no longer any of my business. He is not *my* problem. That works just fine for me. Chris presented a problem, I figured a way to solve that problem, and I took the actions that I believed to be necessary. There was not much more to it than that.

Thinking about the incident these days, I find it interesting that I had found the kubotan on the side of the road while I was walking to school just a week or two before I used it to persuade Chris to leave me alone. It seems fortuitous, does it not? It is almost as if I was *meant* to find the thing. Perhaps that is just silly. I do not care about *that* either. I had the tool, I used it, and it solved the problem of Chris the bully. That is good enough for me. I work with what I have. What else am I supposed to do?

My memory of Chris had become quite distant and vague in the years between attacking him and the sudden loss of my family. After the car accident deprived me of my wife and children, however, this memory became as clear, as distinct, and as insistent as my memories of one day before the accident. I have *many* memories like that. They were dormant, more or less, until the loss of my family in one fell swoop (as the poets say) brought them back into clear focus. Now, many of those memories are extraordinarily clear to me. They no longer allow me to forget them or push them to the "back of my mind," so to speak. I *need* these memories now. They remind me of who I really am and of what I believe needs to be done. They *insist* upon being remembered. For this, I am very grateful. Had I not remembered the incident involving Chris the bully, I might not have taken care of Ed and Travis, or the others. That is why I am grateful for this memory. One day, I may cease to enjoy this gratitude.

Time will tell.

My Third Kill

My third time was *not* "the charm," as the expression has it. This one got a little messy and complicated. That is just the way it goes sometimes, I suppose. It cannot *always* be as easy as was killing "Easy Ed," after all. Murdering people is not *supposed* to be *simple*, I suppose. In any event, the third man I killed caused me a bit more inconvenience than did the first two. I do *not* like being inconvenienced. If I get caught some day, this one might be my undoing, as they say.

Time will tell.

I never learned this man's name, not even his *first* name. It was irrelevant. His behavior was all that mattered. This guy was involved in the nefarious business of trafficking children. If that is *not* sufficient reason to kill him, then the drinks are on me (again). He sold children to people who, presumably, did the most horrible things imaginable to them. Why else would anyone purchase a child behind a truck stop? This guy clearly *needed* killing, in *my* estimation, for whatever *that* is worth. So, I killed him. Any further reasons are superfluous.

He must have been a low-level "player" in the business. If he had been "somebody," then I would probably never have gotten to him. Regrettably, I do not have the wherewithal to kill the evil people with any *real* power or status. Someone else will have to deal with the "big" bad guys. That is a shame, but a man really does need to understand his limitations. I am a low-level vigilante, after all. It is not as if I work for the FBI. My resources are limited. It is actually something of a minor miracle that I found out about this child trafficker in the first place. Maybe I was just in the right place at the right time, as some people like to say. Then again, maybe it is largely a matter of paying attention. Could it be providence, perhaps? It is hard to say. I do not really care.

Regrettably, I was not able to prevent his last "transaction" involving an innocent child, but I hope that his death prevented his participation in future activities of a similar nature. It is impossible to know for certain. A guy who sells a child *once* is probably going to do it again if someone does not stop him, or so it seems to me. Even if the sale I witnessed was his first and only transgression involving children, which is *not* likely, even just *one* deed of this type justifies the death penalty as far as I am concerned. Where my *victims* are concerned, I am the final arbiter of "justice" in their cases. I am judge, jury, and executioner. Try to stop me. Perhaps someone will stop me at some point.

Time will tell.

It had been over two years since I left Travis in the dumpster. Killing people is not a *compulsion* for me. I can stop whenever I want. Yes, that *is* what *addicts* always say, but I actually *did* stop for a good long while. I was busy reading, learning, practicing martial arts, and just living a *seemingly* normal life. When an opportunity presents itself, however, I am generally paying attention. Maybe I just happen to be in "the right place at the right time," as the saying goes. Frankly, I do not really care how these opportunities arise, or whether there is something more going on than meets the eye. Serendipity? What difference does it make?

It seems that a lot of things that should not happen, tend to happen behind truck stop diners. That is not just something from the movies, as I discovered. That is quite real. As it happened on the occasion in question, I had stopped at such a diner, and I had gone to the bathroom just a bit too late to do anything about the child being transferred to the couple who were going to do God-knows-what with him. I did *not save* that child. I doubt I *would* have done so even if I arrived on the scene a little earlier. In all honesty, I am not a courageous man. The trafficker, the truck driver, and the woman with the truck driver probably would have dissuaded me from trying to do something heroic. I am *not*, after all, a hero. The real hero does not subordinate doing the right thing to his own personal interests and he will risk himself to see that justice is done. I did *not* do that. I was afraid. I was hesitant. My fear prevented me from intervening earlier in the unfolding of the event I witnessed. Shame on *me*, I suppose.

I had just finished my breakfast, and I was washing my hands in the diner's restroom, when I heard a child's voice crying, "No!" and the sound of his cry being suddenly and forcefully stifled. There was a small window in the door separating the restroom from the area behind the diner. Someone had taped some thick construction paper over the window, but had done an imperfect job of it. I closed one eye and squinted through the gap that had been left just above the paper, leaving a sliver of window exposed. I saw something that was intended to be concealed from anyone not directly involved.

A smallish Asian man had his hand covering a Hispanic boy's mouth, and he had lifted the boy up on his right hip. He may have been controlling the boy's body with his other arm. From my angle, it was hard to tell. He quickly walked the boy toward a large, fat man standing next to a semi-tractor-trailer truck, or whatever those things are called (the big ones that deliver large shipments). A woman hurried forward, grabbed the child roughly, threw an arm around the kid's neck, and dragged him to the side of the truck that was hidden from my view. The fat man handed an envelope to the Asian guy who had transferred the Hispanic child to the woman. She looked to be of indeterminate race. There was some distance separating us, after all. I could not make out *all* of the details pertaining to the people involved. One can only perceive so much, after all.

The fat guy was white, as far as I could tell. This child clearly did not "belong" to *any* of these adults. None of them were Hispanic, and all the indications of a financial transaction were apparent. What I witnessed was the sale of a human being, as far as I could tell, in any event. Perhaps I could have stepped through that restroom door and tried to save that child. I did not. That might have been heroic. It also might have gotten me killed. People who do those kinds of things tend to carry firearms and other weapons. So, I am clearly *not* a hero. I am, in fact, something of a coward, it seems. There is no way for me to shake that conclusion about myself. I will have to learn to live with that.

I saw the Asian man hurry to a blue Toyota Corolla as the fat man got in the truck. I decided to follow the Corolla. The truck had two people in it, and truck drivers generally carry weapons, even if they are *not* purchasing children. From my angle, I could not get the truck's license plate, and I knew I would not have time to wait for a better angle as the truck left the area, if I wanted to have the opportunity to follow the Corolla. That was all I took into consideration. Instead of following the truck, getting the license number, and alerting the authorities, I decided to follow the small Asian man in the Toyota.

Calling the authorities could lead to questions. Questions could lead just about *anywhere*. I had already killed two people. Answering questions from the police did *not* appeal to me. So, I hurried through the diner, out the front door, and quickly got into my vehicle to get it started. As luck would have it, the Corolla was positioned so that the driver had to circle around the diner and exit the parking lot not far from where I had left my car. The chase was on. Whatever it says about me, I found the idea of the chase exhilarating and exciting. Here was one of those opportunities for which I am always preparing. I saw a man who *needed* killing.

This all happened in Arizona, by the way. I have never lived in Arizona. It was just happenstance that I was passing through on my way elsewhere. It was another stroke of "luck" for me, I suppose. Then again, who knows? Maybe I was *meant* to be in that bathroom so that I could witness the crime. How can I possibly know about such things? The "God's-eye view" is no more available to *me* than it is to anyone else. If there is some grand *plan*, then nobody has told *me* anything about it. I have never received my copy of the *script*. The Road Runner was off and running. *That* was enough to get me following.

I do not know if Asians *deserve* their reputation as bad drivers, but this guy certainly was *not* doing his part to dispel that stereotype. He rode the center line or the "break-down" lane about half the time. The lines on the highway did not seem to have much to do with where this guy drove his vehicle. I witnessed some truly *lousy* driving as I was following this particular motorist. He was probably on the phone or texting, or something like that. Maybe he was under the influence of some intoxicant or other. I cannot know for certain, of course. This erratic driver and I went on our way down the road for a *long* time. We traveled *many* miles along that highway. Eventually, even a child trafficker has to urinate and defecate. As it happens, this guy had to "use the facilities" for the *last* time. I had evacuated my bowels and bladder back at the truck stop. This was all the advantage I really needed. Well, my tire thumper also came in handy again. I *love* that thing!

When he pulled into the roadside rest stop, I continued driving beyond the stop until I saw him exit his Corolla in my rearview mirror. It was not difficult to turn off onto the gravel and drive back to the rest stop after I saw him enter. It is useful to have an all-terrain vehicle for opportunities such as this. Ours were the only two cars in the parking lot. The highway was not particularly busy that day. It was another stroke of "luck," for *me*, anyway. Enough "luck" begins to seem like something occurring by *design*, if one is inclined to think in those terms. What can I say about *that*? The tire thumper was, as *always*, in my driver's side door. I did not even need to look down to grab it as I got out of my vehicle. My hand just *found* the implement on its own. Within a few seconds, I was in the restroom and waiting for the stall door to open. Nobody else was there.

When he emerged from the stall, the Asian guy was looking at something inside his jacket pocket. That made things much easier. Carelessness is a killer. People often pay attention to the wrong thing at the wrong time. On this occasion, his line of sight was directed away from me. He may have *heard* me enter the bathroom, but he did not get a chance to *see* me before I struck. I will never know if he would have put up a good fight. Perhaps he would have proved a more formidable opponent than he looked to be. Neither of us will ever know how mutual combat might have gone. He never had a chance to defend himself. That works just fine for me.

I smashed his skull with all the force I could generate using my tire thumper as a club. When I saw that he braced his fall with one hand, and was, therefore, not unconscious, I slammed the instrument into his head again. That second blow put him down hard and fast. He was *done*. There was suddenly a good deal of blood leaking from his skull. The Asian child trafficker was no longer moving, but his lifeblood was spilling out onto the floor. I gave him another solid whack for good measure. It is best to be as certain as possible in such cases. That final blow led to *more* blood. His head produced a *lot* of leakage. Head wounds tend to do that. I saw an amount of blood that might attract attention. That would *not* work for me. This enterprise had just become even more inconvenient. I *hate* that. It was clear to me that this scene needed to be cleaned up as best I was able, and the whole endeavor needed to be completed fairly quickly. I had no way of knowing whether someone else might be walking into that restroom at any moment. Those rest stops are there for a reason, after all. Drivers feel the "call of nature" just as often as anyone else.

Luckily, this restroom had a *lot* of paper towels. That is not always the case in roadside rest stops. I quickly loaded the body into the trash bag I took from the can in the corner of the restroom. It was not quite large enough to cover the entire corpse, but I got it over his head and most of his torso, to make sure that the rest of the blood leaking from his skull made its way into the bag rather than onto the floor. I slid the bag containing the upper portion of the body away from the pool of blood, and did my best to wipe up and absorb as much of the blood as I could. The bloody paper towels went into the bag on top of this guy's shattered head. Where else was I supposed to put them? Dragging him through the door, I was relieved to see that we were still alone, as far as I could tell. Well, I suppose it was just *me* that was alone at that point. The other guy was dead, after all. Are the dead "alone" when there are no other people in the room with them? That is just an irrelevant semantic quibble, I suppose. Either way, I loaded him into the back of my vehicle, covered him with a large beach blanket, and closed the hatchback. After a few more minutes working with water from the sink and even more paper towels, I managed to make the scene look like there had been maybe a nose bleed or something similarly insignificant. Nobody "investigates" a *little* blood on the bathroom floor of a highway rest stop, right?

I got into my car and continued down the road. Having a body in the rear of my vehicle had not been part of the "plan," insofar as I had thought through the possibilities at all. So, I had to figure out what to do about this situation. One thing I knew for sure is that there would be no "shallow grave" in this guy's future. That is just another stupid cliché. The Asian man was going somewhere *deep*. I needed to find a lake or a quarry, or something similar. Getting rid of a body is a significant undertaking, after all. There is more to say about disposing of the body, but I will get to that later. There is no way of knowing if my efforts were sufficient for me to escape the punishment of man's justice for the crime I committed. Perhaps the corpse will be found, and I will eventually be linked to it. Then again, maybe nobody will ever find that corpse.

Time will tell.

A Promise to My Son

Like any other child, my son was sometimes frightened by the dark. I checked under the bed for monsters on the odd occasion, as do most parents. There were concerns about things that go bump in the night, and lots of other childhood concerns about unseen dangers. It is all fairly standard stuff, as far as I can tell. I also made my son a promise that is probably fairly standard for most fathers. I said, "Don't worry, Daddy will never let anything harm you." Now, of course, my son is *dead*. That means I did *not* keep my promise. Those words have never stopped echoing through my consciousness, and they frequently invade my unconscious mind in dreams (mostly nightmares). I failed to protect my son, and I will never be able to forgive myself for that. There was nothing I could have done to prevent the accident that took my son's life, of course. I was not in the car at the time. That fact, though I understand it fully, provides me with absolutely *no* comfort whatsoever. My boy is dead and I am alive. The details are academic, at best. I cannot undo what has been done. *Nobody* can, after all.

Why did I make a promise that I knew, at some level, I did not have the power to keep? Well, I made that promise because I thought it would comfort my child, and probably because I assumed that I would *outlive* my child. Most parents *do* these days. In other words, I chose the path of least resistance in response to my son's fears. I took the easy way out. Now, I have to pay for that choice until the day that I die. Perhaps I have to keep paying even after I pass away. How can I possibly know whether *anyone* ever gets to *stop* paying for mistakes of that nature? It was just an off-hand remark, and I had good intentions when I made it. None of that means *anything* now. My son died in broad daylight. He was afraid of the dark, but he died with the sun shining. That may be one reason that I have come to prefer the dark. In the bright light of day, there is just far too much that remains visible. There are plenty of things and people to fear in the daylight. The darkness conceals some of those dangers. I find the dark of night vaguely comforting.

As it turns out, it now seems to me that I *am* one of those people that presents a danger in both the dark and the light. The vast majority of the world's population has, of courses, *nothing* to fear from me. I do not kill *decent* human beings, after all. My son probably believed that his daddy would do everything in his power to protect him in the event that some danger might arise. He was correct, if he believed this. What he might not have realized, however, is that *no* daddy has the power to protect his child from *everything*. Fathers sometimes overpromise, it seems. I certainly did. What is any man to do with the knowledge that he failed to protect his child and that the child is now dead? Reflecting on the promise to protect the child, the promise that he did *not* keep, what is any rational adult to do with the fact that his child is dead, in part, because his father was not able to keep him from harm? I have *no* idea what any *other* father might do with this information. With a high degree of confidence, I can claim that I am not the only father, or former father, who must now wrestle with the question of what he is to do with this type of failure. I broke a promise that I had no right to make, and now I must live with the death of the child to whom I made the promise. In *my* case, I must also live with the death of my wife and my other child. What is to be done?

Well, in *my* case, what I *have* done, whether I *should* have done it or not, is kill people whom I despised, at least in part, because they have done terrible, unpardonable things, as far as I am concerned, at any rate, to *innocent* people. Have I merely compounded the amount of suffering in the world? Ultimately, I do *not* believe that I have done so. More importantly, for *my* purposes, I do *not care* whether I have done so. If what I have done is evil or indefensible, then I will have to learn to live with that realization as well, if I ever come confidently to that conclusion. As yet, I have not arrived at any verdict about the matter. Perhaps I will figure this out at some point.

Time will tell.

It is entirely possible that, one day, I will come to regret my actions very deeply. I may even regret my deeds deeply enough that I will feel compelled to turn myself in to the authorities, and face legal punishment for what I have done. Surrendering to the police or the FBI is something I have considered on many occasions over the years. Mostly, I have considered this option because I want to be *done* with the whole affair. Part of me would like to be able to put a period at the end of this story of the former father as vigilante. The terms "vigilance" and "vigilante" must share some common root, I suppose. Both seem to have something to do with paying attention so that one may take some type of crucial action. There is probably more to the semantic relationship than that. Frankly, I do not care enough to devote any time to researching the matter. My whole family is *dead*. I have better things to do with my limited time than investigate etymology. I have people to whom I must attend. There are people that *need* killing. When something needs to be done, someone ought to be willing to do it. In some cases, I have been willing to do what I believed needed to be done. In other cases, I have behaved in cowardly fashion. I am certainly *not* a hero. If I were heroic, then I would be dead or in prison by now. For the time being, I am still "at large" as the authorities like to say. At some point, I may be "at large" no longer. That could certainly happen.

Time will tell.

For what it is worth, I *have* contemplated suicide as a way to bring my story to a conclusion. I own various firearms, after all. It is not difficult for me to get to a high enough bridge or building to be fairly certain that I would not survive the fall. Also, I have studied enough about poison and about drugs to be able to concoct a mixture of ingredients that would be sufficient to kill an elephant or, at the very least, a large, otherwise healthy horse. Reading about such matters is one way that I spend a good deal of my free time these days. I have even put the barrel of a revolver to my temple just to get a sense of whether I would be able to pull the trigger. With a fair degree of confidence, I can report that it would *not* be terribly difficult for me, psychologically and emotionally speaking, to blow my brains out with that gun. I *could* do it.

Ultimately, I think it is very unlikely that I *will* kill myself. First of all, I am not yet convinced that I *deserve* to die. Unless I am confident that a man *deserves* to die, I will not kill that man. I *might* deserve it. It is difficult for me to say so with any great faith. Secondly, and more importantly, suicide seems to me a form of surrender to the world, and an action amounting to letting the world "beat" me does not appeal to me at all. Of course, I am well aware that the world *is* eventually going to kill me one way or another. Nobody gets out alive, after all. It strikes me, however, as something like weakness to do the world's job by my own hand. *It* is going to have to kill me. Nature is going to have to have its way with me, or some other person or persons will have to put me down as I have done to my victims. I will persist for as long as my body functions well enough for me to pursue my ends. My own *end*, as in the end of my *life*, is not something at which I intend to *aim*. Perhaps I will change my mind about this at some point or other. I might put that loaded revolver to my temple and pull the trigger. That is one of the many things that *could* happen. Perhaps I will turn out to be even more of a coward than I think I am.

Time will tell.

Dumping a Body

It is important to be careful about *where* one dumps a dead body, and *when* one does the dumping. I certainly did not want anyone to see me getting rid of the Asian child trafficker, and I do not want anyone to find his body at any point during my lifetime. There is, after all, no statute of limitations on murder. That seems fair to me.

Unlike the previous two cases, I did not have easy access to a lonely river or a large dumpster to make disposal of the body easier. This time, I would have to put in significantly greater time and effort. The dead guy's head and torso were covered with the restroom trash bag, and I had wrapped him up in a large beach towel that was in the rear of my vehicle. So, I was fairly confident that he was not getting blood all over the back of the car under the hatchback. Nonetheless, I did not want to keep him in the back of my vehicle any longer than was necessary. This guy needed to go, but I was not particularly familiar with the area, and no good ideas were coming to me about where I could rid myself of this nuisance safely, or in relatively short order. So, I stopped and bought a map, along with a few other items to make my purchases seem like the kinds of things a tourist might want or need. This was preferable to using a map on my phone, or something similar in the dashboard of my vehicle. Those devices leave digital records, I *think*. No, this would have to be an old-school body disposal. Luckily, my vehicle was designed to be "all terrain," so that expanded my options somewhat. I definitely needed to get a good long way off of the road I had been traveling.

After consulting the map, I realized that I was not too far from a national forest, and it was not exactly the busiest season for visiting such places. I hoped that I would not have to deal with park rangers or other people wandering around in the woods. That would expose me to potential witnesses. That would be inconvenient. If anyone saw me, I would, at the very least, have to dump the vehicle somewhere shortly after the deed was done. That would be another inconvenience. There was no way I was going to kill a witness if I encountered one. First of all, I do not kill *innocent* people. Secondly, I did not need another body in my vehicle and on my list of things to dump in the forest. Why should I make life more difficult for myself, right?

As it happens, I was able to make my way into the park without having to take any main routes or pass by any ranger stations. The off-road performance of my vehicle was pretty impressive. I could have made a compelling commercial for this brand, but that would have been problematic, I suppose. The slogan, "perfect for dumping the bodies of people you have killed," would probably not appeal to the auto maker.

When I had made my way a fairly good distance into the woods, an opportunity presented itself. I am a lucky guy, I guess. There was a large pond, or maybe a small lake, in the national park. What exactly distinguishes a pond from a lake, anyway? That is another investigation I have not undertaken. I stopped near this body of water. After taking a long stroll around the area, and checking to make sure that I was alone (apart from the body in my trunk), I decided to get rid of my problem in the depths of that pond (or lake).

It was important to secure the beach towel with duct tape after I loaded it with enough rocks to ensure that the body would not float back to the surface. Duct tape is absolutely essential for endeavors such as these. Again, I suspect the product was not *designed* for this purpose, but it is useful to "think outside the box," as they say. Even with all of the debris loaded up with it, the body was not quite as heavy as

I had feared it might be. The Asian guy was not a physically large man.

As I searched the body, before disposing of it, I found the envelope he had gotten from the fat truck driver. In retrospect, I realized that he had probably been looking at *that* when I smashed his head in. It contained $20,000. I guess that is what a trafficker got for a young Hispanic boy on the "open market" in those days. What a young boy goes for these days is anyone's guess. I took the money. Why would I *not*? The money, after all, had not done anything to anyone. There is no such thing as "dirty money," but only dirty people who use it for nefarious purposes. Never *blame* the money, I always say.

I waded out into the pond with the body until there was a drop off and I could no longer touch bottom with my next forward step. With a push from the last point where I could still stand, I did something like a modified clean and jerk with the contents of the taped-up beach towel, and I heaved it out away from me as far as I could propel it. The whole thing traveled just a few feet, I guess, but that was sufficient to clear the drop and the child trafficker sank like a bag of rocks. What I had created *was*, essentially, a bag of rocks with a little Asian child trafficker inside of it. The thing plopped into the water and disappeared fairly rapidly. That was all there was to it. He was gone. That was good enough for me.

I took off my wet clothes after I got out of the water, dried myself as best I could manage, and changed into another set of clothes from my suitcase in the back seat. As I indicated earlier, I had just been passing through Arizona, and I had packed a rather large bag for the journey. That came in handy. It seems I am, as I said earlier, a lucky guy.

Time will tell.

A few hours later, I crossed the state line and left Arizona. I have never returned to that state. This should not be interpreted as a derogatory comment about the State of Arizona. It is as fine a place as any other state in the nation. I just prefer to avoid places where I have disposed of dead bodies. It would be irresponsible of me to do otherwise, would it not? Perhaps I have been irresponsible in some way that has not yet come to my attention.

Time will tell.

Four Years Go By

For over four years after I dumped that body in the national forest, I did not kill anyone. That is not bragging, nor is it an indication of a particularly virtuous period in my life, but I simply did not have the opportunity and motive, at the same time, to kill any other terrible people. Probably, I thought I was done with all that. Who needs the aggravation and anxiety, right? A few murders *here*, and a few murders *there*, and pretty soon, we are talking about a *real* criminal history. That might attract attention. That would be inconvenient. I dislike being inconvenienced.

During that period of four years, I grew a full beard, which I had never worn before, and began shaving my head due to the thinning and graying of my hair as I aged. I was not conscious of intentionally changing my appearance for fear of being recognized, but I would guess that anyone who had seen me four years earlier would have had some difficulty identifying me as the same person over the intervening passage of time. Also, I began a powerlifting regime, as much as was possible for a guy my age, and I had put on nearly thirty pounds of muscle (and some middle-aged bulk around the middle as well). So, I was significantly larger, and I had not been a physically *small* man in the first place. My appearance changed significantly.

When I look at pictures of myself from years ago, it seems that I am looking at a different person. I suppose that is a good thing for a "murderer" in the legal sense of the term. Whether my kills count *morally* as murder is, to *my* way of thinking, still an open question. The courts tend to be fairly persnickety about the *letter* of the law, though, so the change to my appearance probably served my interests.

I also did a great deal of reading and research during this four year "lull" in my life. Combing through the *Bible*, the *Quran*, and the *Hadith*, I had tried to convince myself that my actions were righteous in the eyes of my Creator. In all honesty and humility, I cannot claim that my efforts were entirely successful. It is difficult to say. Ultimately, God will judge me, if God exists. Perhaps humans will judge me as well. *Their* opinion does not mean a great deal to me. I have never been terribly impressed with the "wisdom" of *man*. History is, after all, *filled* with human folly. People tend to be poor judges of just about everything. Then again, I am *also* a person, so I cannot trust *my* judgment much either. That is the human condition in a nutshell, I suppose.

Those four years were spent living in various places that were nowhere near any of the locations where I killed people. It seems to me a bad idea to linger too long in the vicinity of a homicide to which I could be connected. That is not terribly unreasonable, is it? I have no desire to go to prison or to be executed. If I am to be captured one day, I have decided that I will confess and spare everyone the necessity of a trial. If, however, I am *not* captured, then I feel no compulsion (most of the time) to just turn myself in. Law enforcement will either catch up with me or they will not. I will just let them do their job where my crimes are concerned, or fail to do so.

Time will tell.

Relationships with other people were few, far between, and very shallow for me during those four years. I had no real desire to get to know anyone very well. Maybe this was because I feared saying something to give myself away. Maybe I just lost interest in most of humanity during that period. In all honesty, I cannot be very sure about what motivated me to avoid the company of humans, for the most part, in those days. It is difficult to know one's own mind. The transparency of my own consciousness and my own reasons are not always easily available to me. Perhaps it is the same for everybody. I do not know everybody. People are something of a mystery, are they not?

I traded in my all-terrain vehicle after cleaning the trunk *very* carefully. The trade-in price was a little disappointing, but I guess I cannot *always* be a lucky guy. Ultimately, I had no complaints about the car. It served my purposes pretty well. Sometimes, I wonder who is driving it now. That person will probably never guess that it had a dead body in the back at one point. Hey, buying a used car is often buying someone else's problem, right? The buyer must beware. Well, the buyer *ought* to beware, at any rate.

Most of my time was spent alone during this period of my life, but I was never really *lonely*. Keeping busy is crucial as far as I am concerned. Every so often, I would show up at a martial arts dojo and learn a few basic striking techniques or brush up on my jiu-jitsu skills. For a guy my age, I think I did pretty well, for the most part. Even some of the younger guys commented that it was challenging to "roll" with me during practices. Perhaps they were just being generous. I do not know.

I avoided becoming a "regular" anywhere, though. Allowing anyone to get to know me well seemed like a bad idea, and I really had no great desire for any close interpersonal relationships. The last one of those ended *very* badly for me, after all. Those who are most dear to us cause us the greatest pain. I think the Buddha said something like that. He was a smart guy. I bet he never trafficked children. Doing so seems like it would be incompatible with the Noble Eightfold Path and the pursuit of Nirvana. Of course, killing people is probably similarly problematic for Buddhists. In any case, I do not subscribe to the entire program where "harmlessness" is concerned. Perhaps I will get there at some point. As for now, I am pretty far from "enlightenment," as the Buddha conceived it, or so it seems to me.

Time will tell.

Also on the topic of "harmlessness," I made sure to spend that four-year period in states that allowed for carrying a firearm without a permit. I was certainly not about to fill out any applications. I was also not going to travel around unarmed. That is another behavior that I find simply baffling. When is anyone better off *not* having a weapon for self-defense? The tire thumper stayed in the driver's side door, but not everything can be handled with a bludgeon, after all. Sometimes, a long-range weapon is desirable. Like a boy scout, I like to be prepared.

As it turns out, having a handgun proved to be particularly useful to me on at least one significant occasion. Those things *really* come in handy for killing people. Sometimes, I think that killing people is the *whole point* of having a firearm. When I hear people say things like, "guns are only good for killing people," I always think, "Were you under the impression that guns are mostly intended for something *else*, you idiot?" Some people, after all, *need* killing. Perhaps I will need a firearm again in the near or distant future. It is one of those things that certainly *could* happen.

Time will tell.

My Wife

I suppose I ought to say something about the woman I took for my bride all those years ago. This subject is more difficult for me to address than most of the others about which I have written so far. Although I loved my wife dearly, she is also, according to all of the available evidence, responsible for the accident that destroyed my entire family, *herself* included, and nobody on this planet has ever caused me as much pain as *she* did due to her stupid mistake on the road. Some might find that to be an unfair or uncharitable characterization. Those people, frankly, have no idea what they are talking about. My wife destroyed my entire family by doing something that is simply *stupid*. *That* information is *not* easy for me to process. My *wife* killed my *whole* family, *and* I loved her deeply. There is bound to be some cognitive dissonance in such a case, is there not?

The crash was clearly an *accident*. There is no question about that. As she was driving our children down a highway, she saw a dead animal in the road. Several witnesses gave the same account. It is very unlikely that they are all incorrect or lying. I am also well aware that my wife always hated running over dead creatures in the road. In fact, she flat out *refused* to do so. *That* was irritating. On more than one occasion, I have had to grab the wheel to prevent her from swerving around a dead animal's carcass and running us into some vehicle in an adjacent lane. On at least *one* of those occasions, the kids were in the car with us. This made me *very* angry. I got so angry, I suppose, because I was terrified by what had almost happened to the entire family. "You could have *killed* us!" I shouted at her. When we got to a place that allowed us to do so, I demanded that she get out and switch places with me. By that point, she was crying and unable to continue driving anyway. So, she agreed to switch.

"What the *hell* were you thinking?" I demanded of her after we had swapped places in the car. "The thing is *dead!* You are *not* going to make it any *deader* by running it over!" For several miles, I "explained" loudly that she was risking the *lives* of our children for the sake of not squashing an animal that was already crushed to a road pancake. How could she be *that* irresponsible and irrational? "What if I had not been here to keep you from swerving?" I insisted. Well, I guess I made my point. Actually, I suppose *she* ended up making my point for me. I was *not* there to prevent her from swerving that last time. Now, I *know* what would happen.

Sure enough, she swerved the car right off of a *mountain* road. I was *not* there to stop her. I was at work. The bills had to get paid, right? The vehicle tumbled down the side of a mountain, rolling as it obeyed the law of gravity, and it smashed, roof first, into a boulder cropping out of the ground hundreds of yards away from the road. The vehicle must have accelerated to impressive speed as it repeatedly rolled over going down that slope. My wife and kids careened down that mountain at sufficient speed to flatten everyone and everything inside of the car upon impact with that gigantic rock. Evidently, the laws of physics were not quite done with the car at that point. It bounced off of the boulder like a number ten can dropped from a rooftop, and it slammed into a grove of trees a little further down the side of the mountain. Unlike in the movies, the thing did *not* burst into flames. It just ended up wedged into that grove somehow. No fire or explosion was necessary. Everybody who mattered to me was dead. They were all *crushed* beyond recognition. My wife *did* that. If that seems uncharitable, then so be it. That *is* what happened.

My whole family died because my wife refused to run over dead animals in the road. They all died because she did something (again) that I had warned her about on many occasions. I always told her to just run over the stupid, crushed animal and protect the *human beings* in the car. Which was more *important*, after all? I told her to protect our *family* no matter what she saw in the road. My wife always said, "I know, I know." Generally, I replied, "If you *know*, then *stop* doing it!" This always made me *very* angry. It must have happened ten times or more. We lived in an area *rich* with wildlife. There was almost *always* something dead on the road. No matter how many times I pointed out the dangers, my wife *always* either slammed on the brakes or swerved when the dead thing was in her lane. She *never* once just ran the damned thing over. She simply could not bring herself to do it. There are, it turns out, consequences for this kind of stubbornness.

I am somewhat ashamed to admit this, but I do *not* think I have forgiven my wife for destroying my family. She was a very kind and gentle creature, my wife. It is precisely because she was so kind and gentle that I fell in love with her, and it is also because she was so kind and gentle that my children are *dead*. Had she survived the crash, I probably would never have forgiven her. I *certainly* would have divorced her. Well, no divorce was necessary (or available). As it happens, she did *not* survive the crash, and I do not know if I will ever be able to forgive her.

Time will tell.

Nonetheless, there is no doubt in my mind that I loved my wife very deeply. There is even a sense in which I *respected* her refusal to drive over dead things in the road. It is, after all, a form of kindness and gentleness. Certainly, I always loved that facet of her character. She would not, as the saying goes, "hurt a fly," even if it landed in her coffee. I cannot say that I still respect her reluctance to run over dead animals. It cost me *everything* that ever mattered to me. A *very* slight ambivalence is the best that I can do.

This is, undoubtedly, one of the reasons that so many people had no idea what to say to me after the accident. Most of them had heard about how the crash had happened. What is there to say to a man who has just lost his entire family because his wife swerved off of a mountain merely to avoid hitting a *dead* animal? I remember one of my wife's friends saying, "She was just such a *kind* person." I had to walk away quickly in order to avoid shouting at that *idiot* about how "kindness," or *squeamishness*, is not *always* a virtue, or, "Yeah, she is so *kind* that she and my children are all *dead!*" When a woman is so "kind" that she destroys her own children, along with herself, maybe we can take a lesson from that. I have not spoken to that stupid, but well-intentioned, woman since the funeral. In all honesty, I hope that I never run into her again. We no longer live anywhere near each other. My wife and children no longer live anywhere. Perhaps we will all be "reunited" in some kind of an afterlife.

Time will tell.

Perversion

Like anybody else these days, I get most of my information from the internet. It does not follow that the internet is a wonderful place to get one's information about the world. There is a wealth of information available, to be sure. Some of it, of course, is *not* true or accurate. It is disinformation or misinformation. Innocent people are routinely accused of heinous deeds, and guilty people are lauded by hordes of admirers who either do not *know* about, or do not *care* about, their various transgressions. Perversions are often treated as virtues in the online environment. That is another baffling feature of modernity. Somebody is probably writing a dissertation on the topic right now. That dissertation will probably be about as worthless as nearly all the rest of them. Does anyone actually *read* those things?

I am well aware that much of the "news" I encounter is nothing more than partisan propaganda, flat out *lies*, and misleading misrepresentations of fact. This is the nature of the contemporary world and the methods of disseminating information about *events* in that world. That, evidently, is just the way it is these days. This is *not* up to me. Not much really *is* up to me, I suppose. There are, however, people who seem, *gleefully*, to take credit for actions that I regard as entirely morally indefensible. A person of this type got my attention one day. He would have been better off if he had *not* gotten my attention. He is *dead* now.

This person was the subject of a floridly positive portrayal for engaging in an activity that I regard as *thoroughly* evil. Indeed, he engaged *regularly* in the kind of behavior that even *Jesus* condemned in the strongest terms. The article went on and on about his *exploits*, without any comment about the degeneracy exhibited by these actions. He would, according to Jesus, as quoted in the *New Testament* at any rate, have qualified as the kind of man who would have been better off "with a millstone hung around his neck and thrown into the sea," than to have lived his life as he chose to live it. Even Jesus was disinclined, by my reading of scripture, in any event, to be forgiving of the type of behavior that lined this guy's pockets. When the "Prince of Peace" condemns a group of people and the behavior in which that group of people engages, it is probably best not to be among their number. If Jesus will not forgive an act, then how likely is it that someone like *me* will tolerate that act gently?

This miscreant was a *stumbling block* throwing himself before the most vulnerable and innocent people among us. Certain elements of our culture's media seem to enjoy *celebrating* the people who engage in this type of conduct. I wish I could get away with killing *those* people in the media as well. Regrettably, my skills, my resources, and the protections enjoyed by most of these mouthpieces make it very unlikely that I could kill any of them and avoid prison or execution. One man can only accomplish so much, after all. Frankly, I find it astonishing that more of the people of this ilk, that is, for reasons I cannot understand, beloved by so much of the "mainstream" media, do not end up bludgeoned to death in a ditch somewhere. We live in distressingly "interesting" times. I believe the ancient Chinese used to issue a curse upon people whom they hated or for whom they had contempt, about living in "interesting" times. I get it. The "interesting" times are generally filled with war, depravity, oppression, and all sorts of other unpleasantness. Moral degeneracy is quite "interesting" these days. In fact, it is so damnably "interesting" that I took it upon myself to destroy one man who made things far more "interesting" in a particular way than should *ever* be tolerated.

Reading various stories from one online publication or another, I found it nearly impossible to fathom the development and expansion of the "fad" in which this person saw fit to participate. Indeed, this guy was being paid handsomely to do something for which I believed he *deserved* to be *killed*. How is it possible that there are people inhabiting "my" culture, "my" society, and "my" nation, who actually *applaud* an obvious effort to facilitate the victimization of children at the hands of the worst people on the planet? When, and *why*, did *this* become "a thing," as the kids say these days? I cannot figure it out. It is one more inexplicable element of the human condition, as that condition is too frequently manifest in its most despicable facets these days. Luckily, for me, I also feel no *need* to figure any of this insanity out. If people wake up tomorrow and start sacrificing their children to the "volcano god," then I will not understand *that* either. If possible, however, there is a good chance that I will try to kill at least one of them. It might be fun to chuck a miscreant into a volcano for the sin of doing the same to a child. Would that count as "poetic justice," or something similar? Hard to say, I suppose.

Researching several sources, it became clear to me that this person, along with distressingly many others, enjoyed a "regular gig" indulging in acts that made me want to eliminate him from a world that contains children in it. As it happens, I *live* in such a world. *He* no longer lives *anywhere*. Had this person ever approached one of *my* children, when they were still alive, I sincerely believe I might have begun indulging in my "new vocation" even if it carried the threat of prison taking me away from my family. That is a counterfactual reality, of course. In the *real* world, my family was already dead and gone when I found out that this degenerate was operating with impunity. That just did *not* work for me.

I took the time to learn as much as I possibly could about this person, his schedule, his place of residence, and any other information that might be useful to me. Regrettably, I learned more than I really wanted to know. This guy, or someone *like* this guy, *needed* to die. This assertion, even today, after the deed has been done, causes me not the slightest moral compunction or hesitation. If Travis deserved to die, and he *did* as far as I am concerned, then the kind of people who do their best to "feed" children to people like Travis also deserved to die, as far as I was concerned.

If someone out there is intentionally infecting dogs with rabies and turning them loose on unsuspecting, innocent people, then someone ought to put a stop to that person or persons. We should not gently tolerate people who knowingly endanger the innocent. If the innocent in question are children, then our "intolerance" may just as well take the most abrupt and decisive form possible. Killing someone like *that* works just fine for me. It astonishes me that there are others for whom it does not "work" just as well as it does for me. The humans are the most *baffling* of all of God's creatures. We are the "sinning" animal, are we not? Something about the big brain seems to allow for the most irrational and immoral behaviors. If there *is* a God, then this must be one of His "mysterious ways" of moving through the world. If there is *no* God, then the evolutionary process cannot be trusted to produce trustworthy big-brained primates, it seems. I do not have any answers where depravity and degeneracy are concerned. *What* is the evolutionary *advantage* of such characteristics and behaviors? In any case, degeneracy and depravity certainly seem to be increasing and metastasizing. I suspect the internet has something to do with this. Perhaps I am mistaken. Honestly, I do not care.

The "virtue" of tolerance *can* easily be overextended. A culture that tolerates degenerates and their depravity is a culture that is unworthy of anyone's concern or allegiance. The culture into which I was born, as far as I can tell, simply does *not* exist anymore. "In *my* day," as old geezers like to say, a person discovered to be in a "line of work" that can only be explained as an attempt to facilitate the efforts of child predators would have ended up in a culvert by the side of the road, the police would have "investigated" the matter for ten seconds or so, and the death would have been declared a "suicide" with no indications of "foul play" discovered. *Nobody* would have protested. There would have been no marches or rioting. Every sane person would have agreed that the miscreant got what he had coming or, at the very least, no sane person would have *defended* the conduct that led to the culvert. What in the *hell* has happened to the nation I once inhabited? Frankly, I think that *tolerance* is the culprit. The collective has decided to sacrifice decency on the altar of misguided "tolerance" for absolutely *everyone*. Well, I hope I will be pardoned for saying so, but not *everyone* ought to be tolerated. I will provide a little friction against this general movement of the culture. Actually, I could not care less whether anyone extends me their *pardon* or not. There are people who *need* killing. I would love to believe that I am not *alone* in this judgment. If I *am*, then so be it. I will remain alone in my efforts unless and until someone else has "had it up to here" just as much as I have. Either that, or I will remain alone in my efforts until someone stops me.

Time will tell.

My Fourth Kill

Maybe it was just as much a matter of *time* as anything else. Maybe I was looking for an excuse to kill again. Frankly, I do not see why it matters one way or another. All I know is that *Sam* showed up on my radar, and he presented me with both a reason and an opportunity to "ply my new trade" again. That term is probably misleading. It is not as if I was getting *paid* to kill people. The $20,000 I got from the Asian guy was a bit of a fluke. Perhaps it served as something like a "finder's fee," but it is not as if anyone gave it to me *voluntarily*, right? This is not "work" that I do "for hire," or at the behest of any person other than myself. I am not a *professional* assassin. This is more like a "hobby" of mine, I suppose. Nobody *hires* me to kill anybody. This is just something that I do for myself. Honestly, I sometimes wonder how many other people do, more or less, the same kind of thing. Surely, I cannot be the *only* one, right? This is a genuine curiosity of mine. Are there not people with advanced skills in this arena, acquired from a military or law enforcement background? I hope someone who is better at this than I am is also "on the job," so to speak. There are, after all, plenty of people out there who *need* killing.

Sam's transgression is not something that I want to mention here. I doubt anybody would fully understand my reasons, or I doubt, at the very least, that anyone would admit *publicly* to understanding my reasons. What he was doing is not even *illegal* in this country. Somehow, it is not even a *crime*! It would be difficult to convince most people, I suppose, that he *deserved* the death penalty. Of course, I did not *need* to convince anybody of anything. Law enforcement could not even have issued him with a citation for his behavior, but he *needed* to die for what he was doing. Is *that* a *paradox*? Maybe not. I do not really care.

Either way, the law was not going to put a stop to Sam's transgressions. No, Sam was engaged in one of those activities that was *once* anathema just about everywhere, but that has become, regrettably, a "normal" part of life in the contemporary Western World. Of course, the fact that people of Sam's ilk are "broadly accepted" (or "tolerated") does not constitute a prohibition on *all* forms of punishment, does it? Given that I *killed* him, it seems that Sam was not "beyond the reach" of justice, after all. He was certainly not beyond *my* reach. Whether justice was or was not done in his case, is less interesting to me than, perhaps, it should be.

I do not take my marching orders from society at large, nor do I pay obeisance to the cultural norms and mores of the day. Look at what a sick and degenerate society I inhabit. Why the hell would I want to be "in tune" with this modern Babylon? No, to *hell* with that. Some things are perfectly legal, but entirely intolerable nonetheless. God will be my judge, I suppose. If there is *no* God, then there is even *less* reason to be concerned about what other people have to say on the topic of moral legitimacy. Who the hell are other people? They are just talking primates with *constructs* for consciences if there is no God. *That* does *not* impress me.

Sam lived in Oregon when he came to my attention. I have *never* lived in Oregon. Now, I never *will* live there. Sam no longer lives anywhere. According to the *official* account, Sam committed *suicide*. I know better. Anyone reading this may or may not figure out what really happened, and to *whom* it happened. It would be foolish of me to use my victim's *real* name in this case, would it not? I will call him "Sam," but the name he actually used is far more "stylish" and polysyllabic. It even included a royal "title" of sorts. I should not reveal any more than that. Well, I probably should not reveal *any* of this, but something impels me to tell the tale as best I am able. This memoir really might land me in prison.

Time will tell.

I read a story about Sam on the internet (God *love* it). Does anyone get their information anywhere else these days? Sam died just a couple of years ago. He died because I killed him (the "suicide" account notwithstanding). One of the things I learned during the years after I dumped that body in Arizona involved methods of breaking into a house or apartment without leaving any sign of a break-in (or leaving, at the very least, *minimal* and *inconclusive* indications of a break-in). Unfortunately for Sam, his home was not exactly well-fortified against intruders. Even a relative novice like me found it fairly easy to get in without breaking a window, kicking in a door, or making very much noise, or causing very much visible damage, at all. Sam did not have a dog. That made things *much* easier. It is difficult to get past a dog. They are called "man's best friend" for good reason.

The first two nights of my "stakeout," I did not see Sam leave his home at night. So, I just remained parked at a distance that allowed me to observe his house, as well as the area surrounding it, and I also took some notes that might prove useful to me when Sam finally decided to venture out for a night on the town. The third night *was* the charm this time (for *me*, at any rate). Sam did not return home until after 2 a.m. Evidently, Sam was something of a night owl. He liked to burn the midnight oil. I could throw in other euphemisms or metaphors, I suppose, but those two will do. Sam never left his house under his own power again. He left only one more time, and he went out feet first on that occasion (I suspect).

Many Americans have a pretty clearly designated "television chair" in the living room. We watch all too much television, in my opinion. It simply is *not* healthy. It is particularly unhealthy when a man is hiding in your home with a handgun. Sam "committed suicide" with a revolver I had purchased many years earlier in a state on the other side of the country. It certainly *could* have made its way into Sam's possession by the time I shot him in the head with it. In any event, it would be very difficult for anyone to prove that Sam had *not* acquired the thing. Actually, it would probably be a practical *impossibility* to do so. Moreover, nobody has had any reason to even *wonder* about whether Sam did not actually own the weapon in question (as far as I can tell, at any rate). The scene looked like the scene of a suicide, because I did my job properly and carefully.

Gloves are crucial for this type of endeavor. Leaving finger prints and DNA around Sam's house could have caused me a variety of inconveniences. I do *not* like to be inconvenienced. Even though I have *no* criminal record (consider *that* for a moment), it still would have been unwise to leave any more clues to my presence at the scene of the "suicide" than could have been reasonably avoided with a bit of diligence. This one was quite likely to make the news, and I did not want to become part of any story that emerged in subsequent days.

It is not at all difficult to obtain gloves that are more or less indistinguishable from the ones that surgeons use. I have *boxes* of them. Any "big box" store carries these things. Plenty of online outlets have them as well. I have no idea why more criminals neglect to pick up at least a few pairs of them. If one wishes to commit crimes and get away with it, then one really ought to be willing to make at least *this* tiny investment. In any case, I wore them when I broke into Sam's house.

The place I chose to hide upon Sam's return home was ideally located to conceal me, and also to give me a quick and simple path from my hiding place to Sam's television chair. This is a result of my diligence, I suppose. A good hiding place is pretty important for pulling off a fake suicide. I guess Sam decided to watch some late-night entertainment before he turned in for the evening, because he plopped down in that chair and turned on a movie within just a few minutes of coming home and dropping his stuff just next to the stairs. I could describe the stuff he dropped there, but that would be inadvisable. Most *men* do not own these items. Men really *should not* own these items, but I will leave the matter right there.

Sam was pretty clearly under the influence of something or other. Maybe it was alcohol. Maybe he had taken some "recreational" drug or other. Probably, it was a combination of intoxicants. In any event, Sam was clearly not as "sharp" and attentive as he could have been. That came in handy. Intoxicants *are* killers, after all. Carelessness is another. I ought to know.

Two quiet steps brought me quickly to the back of the chair into which Sam had lowered himself. I understood that it was crucial to fire from an angle that could plausibly serve for a self-inflicted gunshot wound to the head. In one swift motion, I raised the revolver to Sam's head and pulled the trigger just before the barrel made contact with Sam's right temple. Most people are right-handed. I played the percentages.

The opposite side of Sam's head seemed to *explode*. The exit wound must have been fairly significant. I did not take the time to look at it very carefully. It is best not to pause and "admire one's handiwork" in such instances. As quickly as I was able, and without disturbing anything too much, I took Sam's right hand and slipped the trigger finger where it needed to be, wrapped his other fingers around the weapon beneath the trigger, and let his hand drop in the hope that police would see the position of his body as the likely result of a suicide. As it turns out, they did (as far as I can tell).

Leaving the house, I was careful to avoid the blood spatter area, and I left through the same side door in the garage that had allowed me access to the house. People often forget to lock that door. Sam forgot. That cost him. The door separating the house and the garage is generally the easiest lock to defeat. As it happened, Sam had not even bothered to lock *that* door either. His big, rolling, external garage door was locked, after all. The side door to the garage, however, was not. That was enough to get me to the *internal* garage door to the house. Sam left that one unlocked also on the night in question. Is that not just sloppy and irresponsible? How easy did this guy want to make it for those who would do him harm? It is hard to say. In any event, he never got a chance to learn his lesson about securing his home. That is just how it goes sometimes.

When I got outside, I saw nobody moving about at that hour. It was *late*, after all. Walking a few blocks got me to my vehicle, and I drove away being careful not to exceed the speed limit, run any stop sign, or violate any other rules of the road. Breaking the law as I left the scene of a murder (later ruled a suicide) would have been unwise. There is no excuse for carelessness in this kind of situation. Carelessness is a dangerous habit of mind. Sam was careless. Sam is *dead*. His death was ruled a suicide, but no culvert was involved, and I suspect the authorities actually did their job as best they could. There were simply no indications of "foul play" at the scene. That is because I was *not* careless.

I drove for hours before I felt compelled to stop and use the restroom. There was a gas station with an attached convenience store not far from the border with Idaho. The border with Nevada was much closer to the scene of the crime. *That* is why I drove to Idaho. After I filled my tank, I went in and got a large coffee. With the caffeine in my system, I was able to keep driving through most of the subsequent day. By the time I stopped at a roadside motel, I was not very far from Wyoming. It is worth pointing out that I did *not* live in Wyoming at that time. It is best to avoid driving *straight* home from the scene of the crime, or so it seems to me. Besides, there is a lot of *beautiful* country in that area. I enjoyed taking the scenic route back to the home in which I lived at that time. I live nowhere near there today.

After many more miles slipped by, I stopped at a library about an hour away from my home to check the news from Oregon. Sam was definitely dead. There was, at that time, no mention of the cause of death, and no mention of "foul play," as the expression has it. Why would such a possibility even occur to the authorities?

There was no viable alternative to being patient about the matter. Eventually, I *did* see another news blurb about Sam's death, and it was reported that he had "taken his own life." Interestingly, some of Sam's acquaintances reported that his "suicide" was not particularly surprising. He was, according to those who knew him well, something of an unstable character. He had struggled with depression for years. Another stroke of *luck* for me, I suppose.

At any rate, after grabbing another cup of coffee in the town where I had stopped to check the news the first time, I simply drove the rest of the way home. That drive took many hours. My *work* was done as far as Sam was concerned. A bit of rest would be the next order of business. The whole affair had been quite draining for me. Murder can take a physical and psychological toll, it seems. Perhaps that is the way it *should* be. I am more interested in the way things *are* than in the way they *should* be. I live in the *real* world, after all.

There is no way for me to predict, at this time, whether I have or have not executed my final victim. There have been no others since I put Sam down like another rabid dog. Perhaps I will find "just cause" again at some point or other. There are, after all, *plenty* of terrible people in the world. Sometimes, I get a little restless. The temptation to kill is stronger on some occasions than it is on others. Perhaps the temptation will prove sufficient to move me to get rid of another terrible person at some point or other.

Time will tell.

My Cowardice

A young man at one of the dojos I visited revealed a disturbing story about an acquaintance of his when we were chatting one day. It is not as if I *never* speak to anyone. That conversation got me to consider deploying my new "craft" regarding another particularly terrible person. Ultimately, I let this one go. In the final analysis, I could not figure out how to kill this particular reprobate and get away with it. I do *not* wish to go to prison. As I have indicated, I am not heroic at all. In fact, I am at least as cowardly as anyone else. I cannot kill *everyone* who needs killing. Ultimately, I probably cannot even kill enough of those people to make a significant difference at a societal level. It would be quixotic to suppose otherwise, and I am, in the final analysis, not even as much of a hero as the titular character who "tilted at windmills" as if his *soul* depended upon fighting those hopeless battles. I do not want to "fight the unbeatable foe," and I accept the fact that this makes me something of a chicken. *Don Quixote* was, after all, a bit of a lunatic. Sometimes, I wish I were as nobly crazy as that *Man from La Mancha*. I am not. It is possible that I am not *crazy* at all. How am I supposed to know the fact of *that* matter?

The man about whom my younger acquaintance from the dojo told me was, according to the account I heard, a drug dealer. My young acquaintance met this man because he was interested in trying performance-enhancing supplements to give him an edge in developing his skills and his body to be more effective in the mixed martial arts career he intended to pursue. This kid was a pretty good fighter for someone his age, but he thought that he was somewhat underdeveloped physically. He hoped that steroids, or some other type of chemical enhancement, would enable him to work harder, recover more rapidly, and thereby assist him in becoming a successful professional fighter.

He was, however, concerned about some of the other projects in which this purveyor of performance-enhancing drugs was also engaged. It is not clear to me why this dealer told my acquaintance about the other drugs that he sold. Maybe he hoped to spread the word about the availability of his products. Perhaps he hoped that this aspiring mixed martial arts fighter might also be interested in some more "recreational" drugs as well as the performance-enhancing products that he offered. I do not know enough about the "drug game" to have a clear sense of how these guys generally function. I have never been very interested in drugs from either category. I distrust narcotics and pharmaceuticals in general. That makes me something of an "old fogey," I suppose. That works for me.

As is often the case, I suppose, where the sale of illicit drugs is concerned, this particular dealer was connected to organized crime. His full "status" relative to organized crime in general never became clear to me, but he was, at the very least, "an associate," in some sense. In addition to the drugs that attracted prospective athletes, this guy also sold the kinds of narcotics that were not particularly "performance enhancing" where athletic careers are concerned. He also dealt cocaine, methamphetamine, heroin, and MDMA (which was called "ecstasy" or "x" when I was younger). Evidently, the "cool kids" call it something else these days. I have no idea why that should be so.

His method of acquiring customers, as it was recounted to me, was giving young people, sometimes *very* young people, free samples of these drugs in order to get them hooked on the "high" they could experience. When they sought him out looking for more frequent access to that "high," then, of course, there were no more *free* samples to be had. The young people had to start *paying*.

In some instances, so I am credibly informed, the young people who did not have enough *money* to purchase their drugs of choice were permitted to "pay" with "services" to this dealer and his associates. The types of "services" that young people can offer tend to be fairly limited. They mostly paid with their *bodies*. They paid, ultimately, with what I will call their "souls," or with that essence of *youth* that tends to be prized by perverts, degenerates, and predators who exploit the vulnerable for their own gratification. In other words, many of this dealer's "clients" became prostitutes to be passed around among his associates in the world of organized crime, and among the people they sought to use for various purposes and advantages. There was at least one story of a politician who liked young boys, and whom the criminals now "owned," because they could reveal this to the public or the authorities any time they wanted to do so. This politician, I was told, voted as the "syndicate" told him to vote on legislation. The children prostituted to this politician were used for leverage and extortion. Regrettably, arrangements of this nature appear not to be at all unusual where the drug trade is involved. Girls and women do not always need money to feed their drug habits. Sometimes, boys and young men make the same exchange. It is generally difficult to determine just how "high up" the corruption extends. Democracy as "rule by the people" is, at the very least, something of an oversimplification. Many elected representatives have little or no interest in representing the desires of the general *public*. They vote in accordance with the interests of the powers that "own them" as the result of campaign contributions, or as the result of the predilections about which they desperately want the public *not* to know. Someone *always* knows. *That* someone is the party whose interests that politician will represent, like it or not. That, however, is a bit of a digression, is it not? I am not a very talented writer. Back to *basics*.

For some time, I observed this dealer after my young acquaintance pointed him out to me one day as we were leaving the dojo. When I could manage to do so without too much risk of being noticed, I followed him to a few of his favorite haunts.

This was not something I did regularly or, as it turns out, for a very long time. People in his line of work often have *other* people following them as well. Some of those who follow the drug dealers are law enforcement. Others are their "associates" involved in various criminal enterprises. The "associates" like to keep tabs on people who could cause them problems with law enforcement, I suppose. On *one* occasion, it became clear to me that I had been noticed by a person who was either a criminal or an undercover law enforcement official *posing* as a criminal. It is important to pay attention when one is engaged in surveillance. In either case, I did not wish to be noticed more than once by either of those two types of observers. It would have been very dangerous and undesirable if anyone started paying attention to *me*. Murderers generally try to avoid too much attention.

This one instance of being noticed, which was the only instance of which I was *aware*, but not necessarily the only instance that had occurred, was sufficient to dissuade me from pursuing the matter any further. Killing a drug dealer who pimped out young people as a form of barter for their fixes would have been a worthwhile project, but I was not willing to jeopardize my life or my freedom to accomplish this particular assassination. I am no hero. I chose the cowardly option of walking away and letting the whole nefarious enterprise unfold without my intervention.

Perhaps I *could* have alerted the authorities about this poisoner and defiler of the youth. The thought crossed my mind briefly, but *only* briefly. Murderers like myself could very easily run into "entanglements" resulting from any such contact with the authorities. I do *not* like inconveniences involving law enforcement. The "inconvenience" of spending the rest of my life in prison is particularly unappealing to me. So, I did *nothing* about this drug dealer. I failed to remove him from the face of the planet. Shame on me *again*, I suppose.

He appeared at the dojo a few more times before I stopped going there. I do not go *anywhere* more than a few times if I can help it. To the best of my knowledge, this drug dealer paid no attention to me. He seemed to be far more interested in other "demographic groups" with which I had fairly little association. He never approached me with any offer. All things considered, that is for the best, I guess. Well, it is for the best as far as my *primary* interests are concerned.

Thus, I learned conclusively that my primary interests are *not*, in fact, "seeing that justice is done," or "giving malefactors what they deserved," but, like just about everybody else, my real interests are mostly *selfish*. My "moral sensibilities" took a backseat to self-preservation. In this way, I realized that I am at least as bad as those people for whom I often feel contempt. That was a particularly jarring, but not a particularly surprising, realization. I always suspected that there was nothing particularly special about me and my interests. I am just a man, after all.

It would not have been at all difficult for me to run up behind that drug dealing pimp and split his head open with something heavy and solid. I could easily have rammed a knife into his back and put an end to him in public and in broad daylight. Shooting him to death would have been even *easier*. I did *none* of those things, though. Witnesses would have seen me, and I would have been caught or killed. Those were prices that I was unwilling to pay in order to "do the right thing," as I understood my moral duty regarding this terrible person. I shirked my moral obligations, and I have done so countless times both before and after I became aware of this particular miscreant. In fact, it seems a safe bet that I have shirked more moral obligations than I have fulfilled. That makes me about as pathetic as anybody else, I suppose. No, I am certainly no "avenging angel," or anything remotely like one. It seems that I am just another bit of human detritus polluting the planet with my weakness and selfishness. *Hoorah* for the human race.

It is difficult to place myself with any exactitude on a moral continuum. Am I morally superior to drug dealers, pimps, and those who prey upon the innocent? Well, I *hope* that I am. Am I morally *inferior* to the people who are willing to risk life, limb, and freedom to do the right thing? Yes, I am *certainly* inferior to *those* people. In fact, I suspect there are people who would be entirely morally justified if they found out how I have lived my life and decided that *I needed* killing. If I had to defend my life before a tribunal of angels and saints, then I could do no better than confess my cowardice, throw myself on the mercy of the court, and hope *not* to get what I probably deserve. Perhaps I will be compelled to do something like that at some point. I suppose I expect to "face the music" sooner or later.

Time will tell.

My Daughter

She was not even two years old when she died. My daughter still had to be in a car seat when either of us drove her anywhere. Under the circumstances of the crash, that child car seat did her *no* good at all. Nobody makes a car seat that can withstand tumbling down the side of a mountain and slamming upside-down into a giant rock. It is quite probable that nobody ever *will* make one *that* sturdy. Even NASA cannot make something *that* formidable, I suspect.

My daughter was "the apple of her daddy's eye," as the common expression has it. There was nothing unique about our relationship as far as fathers and young daughters are concerned. Nearly all fathers love their young daughters and would do just about anything for them. Nearly all young daughters love their daddies, and they look to their fathers as examples of what men are supposed to be. The little girls begin doing this long before they become *aware* that they are doing this. That is why it is so important for fathers of daughters to behave in the way that they would want the men who enter their daughters' lives in the future to behave. Fathers serve as the archetype of manhood in the minds of their little girls. So, fathers had *better* try to be good role models.

Most fathers, I suspect, want their daughters to grow up and marry men who are at least as virtuous as their fathers, and who will protect and defend their daughters if and when they are in danger. It is a father's obligation to *be* the man by reference to whom she will judge all other men who might wish to become part of her life. This is one of the fundamental moral duties of the father. He must model the behavior that he wants his daughter to value, and to admire in other men. My daughter died, and now I periodically *kill* people. Although she can no longer observe my behavior, at least not in the way she once did, I cannot help but conclude that I have *failed* in my moral duty to be a virtuous man, the *kind* of man that I would want my daughter to marry when she grows up. Even if I *may* have been justified in killing the men that I have destroyed, I still would *not* want my daughter to have grown up to marry a *murderer*. I would *not* want my daughter to end up marrying a man like *me*, in other words. That is a disturbing fact, and I struggle with what I have done, in large part, because I know that I am *not* a good enough man for my daughter. I am *not* the kind of man that I would have wanted my little girl to bring home when she became a woman. She will *not* become a woman. She will not even have the opportunity to make the mistake of choosing a man like her daddy. *That* is *failure*.

My daughter will certainly *not* grow up to make the mistake of marrying a man like me. My daughter will not grow up to marry *any* man at all. She is in a casket, buried in the soil next to her mother and her brother as well. Everything that my daughter could have grown up to be, to do, and to experience, is now irrelevant to all of the people who will never know that she ever existed. Any children to whom my daughter might have given birth will never exist. My grandchildren are *fictions* now. If any person dies as a child, then all of their potential descendants are eradicated. Their potential becomes irrelevant to everyone else on the planet, as far as anyone knows or will ever fully understand. All of those potential people will never happen, and all of their potential experiences will never be realized. That is just *part* of what it means when a person dies as a child. If *that* is not tragic, then the drinks are on me, and I will buy a round for everyone who *never* got to be born into our world. I can afford *that*.

My wife swerved to avoid driving over a *dead* animal, and that act erased my daughter's future. It also erased my son's future. It erased my wife's future as well. Perhaps that analysis seems petty and unfair. I suppose that is another of my weaknesses and failings. Evidently, I am something of a petty man. That is just one more fact that, I suppose, I am going to have to learn to accept about myself. I am the kind of *petty* man who tends to focus on what has been *lost*, at least where the lives of my loved ones are concerned. Perhaps I will learn to "move on" at some point in *my* future. Of course, that is only a possibility because I am not *dead* yet. It seems that I still *have* at least *some* future to live. I was not in the car on the day of the accident. Had I been in the car, then my entire family might still be alive. Some might suggest that I ought to learn to "make peace" with the world as it stands. I have not yet managed to do so. Perhaps I never will.

Time will tell.

Reasons and Motives

We generally try to assign purpose or motive for crimes. Prosecutors usually find it difficult to secure a conviction if they cannot explain *why* the defendant allegedly committed the crime for which a trial has become necessary. People do things voluntarily for *reasons*. This is a staple of any analysis of human behavior. We have purposes for what we do. Sometimes, our purposes are not entirely clear, even to the person performing the act in question, but we always assume that *some* purpose *must* be at work. I have certainly made this assumption about all of the deeds I have described here. Considering the matter at this moment, however, I cannot help but wonder whether this general assumption is not mistaken or oversimplified in some cases. In particular, I have begun to have my doubts about *my* motives for killing the people I have mentioned here. They were terrible people. Of that, I have *very* little doubt or uncertainty. It does *not* bother me that they are dead.

Something else *does* trouble me, though. Did I kill Ed, for example, merely because I wanted him to die, or did I kill him because I also needed his killer to be *me*? These are separate (or *separable*) questions. I have read about murderers being executed, and I have done so without being aware of any *envy* toward the executioners. In nearly all cases, I have been comfortable that the person executed ended up *dead*. I experienced no *yearning* to have participated in the process.

Most people can identify a reason for any particular act anyone might mention. Ask a man why he goes to work, and he is likely to mention making money and, if he is fortunate, he may also mention something about the satisfaction he derives from some facet of his occupation. Ask a man why he goes to a football game or a baseball game, and he will probably tell you something about why he *enjoys* the experience, and something about why *this* team is his favorite as opposed to *that* team. Everyone is accustomed to these types of reasons explaining these general sorts of behaviors.

When I consider *my* reasons for *killing* people, however, I cannot easily resort to explanations involving some material benefit, or any intrinsic enjoyment of the experience, or even to anything like the pursuit of "justice," or the nearest approximation that I can manage. None of that adequately explains my motives for killing people, at least as far as I can tell.

I cannot, for example, kill anyone because he is responsible for destroying my family. The party who is probably responsible is already dead, and I would *never* have killed *that* person under any circumstances that I can readily imagine. I *loved* my wife dearly. Although I *do* hold her responsible for the accident, and I might not be able to forgive her, there is no chance that I would have believed she *deserved* to die for refusing to run over a dead animal in the road. I could never have believed that *she* needed killing. The men I *have* killed had absolutely *nothing* to do with my family or that accident.

As for whether the men I have killed *deserved* to die, I am sometimes inclined to answer in the affirmative without hesitation. In other moods, however, I am somewhat more hesitant and circumspect about the matter. Were these people mentally ill to one degree or another? It is, obviously, somewhat difficult for me to say that they either were or were not. Indeed, Sam is the one to whom I am mostly likely to ascribe mental illness or cognitive dysfunction. Mentally healthy men simply do *not* do what Sam chose to do for a living.

Travis clearly suffered from some condition that caused him to attach sexual desire to children. That has *got* to be an illness of some kind, right? Ed and the Asian man, upon surface inspection, just appear to be terrible people who subordinate the interests of others to their own greed or self-aggrandizement. Is *that* a mental illness? I do not *know* that it is *not*. I do not know that it *is*. Also, I know almost *nothing* about the *rest* of the lives lived by the men I have killed. It is *possible* that they also had countervailing *admirable* attributes. Maybe the *only* thing I knew, or confidently *believed*, about any of these men was, in each case, the *very worst* thing I could have learned about each of them. Maybe Ed, for example, donated lots of money to charity and was really fun at parties. Who knows?

I have had plenty of time, over the years, to contemplate the possibility that I have killed deeply flawed people who, for one reason or another, could *not* have *prevented* themselves from becoming the kinds of people who did the things I observed them doing. Frankly, I am not at all clear about whether people even have *free will* or can be held legitimately morally responsible for *anything* that they do, or that they believe. The best philosophers and neuro-scientists have *not* settled *those* questions. Who the hell am *I* to render judgment in *that* area? Do human beings have free will? Should they be held morally accountable? I do not know, but I cannot seem to help thinking of them as if they *are* responsible for the things that they do.

Ultimately, I think that I do not really *care* very much about free will, moral accountability, or whether I have been just or fair in my actions toward these men. In other words, I do not really care whether they *deserved* to die. Even if someone had convinced me that *none* of them deserved to die, I suspect I would have killed *all* of them anyway. I *wanted* them dead. I killed them *because* I wanted them dead. There may not be much more to the explanation of my motives and reasons than that. So be it.

The question of *why* I wanted them dead asserts itself at this point. If I did *not* want them dead because I believed that they *deserved* to die, then what is the reason, what is my *motive*, for *wanting* them to die, and for wanting to be *the one who killed them*? I cannot claim that if I failed to kill them, then nobody and nothing else would do it. Indeed, the *world* absolutely *would* do it, sooner or later. None of them were immortal, at least not in *bodily* form. *Nobody* gets out of this world alive. Why did I not simply "allow nature to take its course," rather than going to all the time, trouble, and considerable *risk* involved in dispatching them *myself*? I do *not*, as I have indicated, want to go to prison. Frankly, the thought of spending the rest of my days in prison scares the hell out of me, when I allow myself to consider the possibility at any length. Nonetheless, I *did* kill these mere mortals who may or may not have deserved their execution. I was not content to allow someone or something *else* to put an end to these people. *I wanted to kill them myself.*

The best I can do to answer the question of *why* I have done *what* I have done, or even to *approach* the question, is to fall back on the dark impulses that lurk, I assume, within *every* man. When I had a wife and children about whom I had to be concerned, my violent impulses were largely held in check. I was unwilling to risk the welfare of my family just for the sake of satisfying the urge to harm people who roused the "strike-back" reflex in me. Hardly a day goes by, hardly a day has *ever* gone by, on which I have not encountered someone doing something that made me want, at least for a moment, to strike at that person. The "strike" could be merely a verbal outburst, as is the case with most unpleasant encounters on the highway, for example. There is relatively little risk associated with cursing in the privacy of my car. In other cases, I experience a strong urge to punch a man or beat him with some implement, but I typically decide that the associated risks are not worth the experience of the assault. I assume this is a fairly standard part of the male psyche. Most men want to hit people, but *refrain* from doing so (for the most part).

So, how is it that I *resist* the urge to *punch*, and often resist the urge even to *speak* in an unpleasant fashion, but I have *failed* to resist the urge to *kill* men on *four* separate occasions? Clearly, the risks associated with murder outstrip the risks of verbal jousting or a fistfight. *Why* have I been willing to *kill*? Why have I *needed* to kill?

The dark impulse, I suspect, finds greater satisfaction in *killing* than it does in any alternative action that fails to eradicate the *object* of that urge. The thought of simply beating Ed into unconsciousness did not *move* me. Indeed, I never regarded it as a truly *viable* or satisfying option. Instead of slamming my tire thumper into his skull, I could easily have used the thing to break his legs. If I had opted to deliver a non-fatal beating to Ed, then he could have gone to the authorities, I suppose, and I might have faced legal punishment. It would, however, have been a case in which the *evidence* would have been nothing more than *his* word against *mine*, in any *court*, or in the judgment of the police. *How* could I have been convicted? Why would that case even get to trial? Ed could not have proved that his legs were broken by *me*. There were *no* witnesses. Would I have faced *any* punishment at all? Probably not.

Was I concerned that if I left Ed alive, then he might have sought some type of private retribution? Was I concerned that his brothers, or his buddies, might find me and my family? Not really. He and I never met, and never spoke. He would have had no way of even *finding* me. That is a point that also applies to potential *legal* consequences. Ed would not have been much more likely to "catch up with me" if I had just broken a few of his bones as opposed to *killing* him. The assault would have been a baffling and inexplicable event from his point of view. That would have been an *end* of the matter. At some level, I am sure I understood this at the time. Yet, I chose to *kill* rather than *wound* him. My best guess is that a mere beating would have been insufficient to satisfy my urge where Ed, and the others I have mentioned, are concerned. I wanted them *dead*, and I wanted it to be *me* that *made* them dead. I did not want them merely to *suffer*. Indeed, none of them *did* suffer very much. For the most part, they had no idea what hit them, and they died quickly.

My desire to *kill*, unfettered by concerns about the possible consequences for anyone other than *myself*, was sufficient to "trip the switch," and I killed because I *wanted* to kill, and I was reasonably confident that I could do so without getting *caught*. I wanted to do it, I was able to do it, so I did it. That is all. When I sift through all of my *reasons*, only *that* survives the process of investigation and interrogation. Justice be *damned*.

It makes no difference to me whether my victims were morally blameworthy or not. Each of them did something that "tripped the switch," and each of them was unfortunate enough to do so at a time, and under circumstances, that allowed me to be optimistic about getting away with killing them. *That* is the best I can do to explain my *reasons* for what I have done. My basic motive is an inherent element of the human condition, as far as I can tell. It may be a stronger and more prevalent condition among males of the species than among females, but I do not care enough about the differences between the sexes where violence is concerned to expend much time or effort trying to disentangle the divergence between motives and reasons for men as opposed to women. I have never *been* a woman. I do not *care* what drives women where violence is concerned. That subject has nothing to do with *me*.

If I had never met my wife, never had children, and never developed any close connections with other people, or the type of connections to which familial relations give rise, then I suppose I might have started killing people much earlier than I did in the *real* world. When I smashed that kubotan into Chris' skull when I was a child, he could easily have *died* as a result. I was certainly *not* being careful to *avoid* killing him when we were both just kids. So, maybe I have *always* been the dangerous creature that I now recognize myself to be. It is entirely possible that meeting my wife, and making a family with her, forestalled my transition to becoming a killer for years or decades. Perhaps I would have been one of those guys who shows up in those documentaries about "men who murder," and I would have been interviewed in prison while I served a life sentence. What story would I have told an interviewer about *why* I killed people, if the conditions of my life had been vastly different? There is no way to know how I might have turned out in different circumstances, I suppose. It is notoriously difficult to inspect the specifics of *counterfactual* worlds. That is probably because those worlds do *not exist*.

Does it really matter how I *might* have turned out if events and conditions had unfolded differently than they did, in fact, unfold? My life is not "as it might have been," unless it could *only* have been one way. The world is as it *is*, and not as it allegedly "*might* have been." My experiences stand (or fall) on their own. Counterfactuals are irrelevant. Maybe things could have been otherwise. Maybe we will find out that nothing could have happened any differently. Perhaps I will understand the facts of these matters better at some point.

Time will tell.

Death

There are, broadly speaking, only *two* possibilities regarding the nature of human death. Either the person ceases to exist upon bodily death, or the person does *not* cease to exist upon bodily death. That disjunction seems to cover just about all potential results of a person's bodily death, does it not? One ceases to be, or one persists. The nature of an afterlife, if there is an afterlife, can take indefinitely many forms, but there is either *some* afterlife, or there is not. A tautology is difficult to dismiss, or so it seems to *me*, at any rate. A thing either *is*, or it is *not*.

From this observation, it seems to follow that my victims either continue to exist in some post-mortem form, or they no longer exist at all. If I am to be honest, then I must confess that I hope the latter is the case for the men whom I have killed. I hope that they do *not* exist anymore. Unfortunately, if that is true of my victims, then I must assume that it is also true of my *family* as well. That thought is *far* less appealing to me. I would like to believe that my wife and children are in heaven, or will be reincarnated, or that they continue to have some form of experience or other, but I do not "like to believe" the same thing about the men I have murdered. My guess is that I *cannot* have it *both* ways. It is, I suppose, *possible* that *evil* people cease to exist when they die, but *good* people enjoy some form of post-mortem persistence. Even for those who are inclined to embrace belief in a good and just God, this possibility *must* seem like a bit of wishful thinking. At any rate, this particular potential form of "justice" strikes *me* as nothing more than an appeal to magic. Human beings are not *that* different from one another, are they? No, I strongly suspect that either *everybody* has an afterlife, or that *nobody* does. That seems most plausible to me. If I am correct about this, then what follows about what I have done by killing the people I have mentioned here? Well, *that* is a difficult and uncomfortable question to ponder.

I want them to be dead and *gone*. What I *want* is almost certainly irrelevant to the way that things *are*. If the men that I have killed are still "out there" somewhere (or in some *sense*), then all I have accomplished is their removal from the living population of this planet (for the time being). Do they still have the same *character* in the afterlife? Are they still doing terrible things, but just doing those things in some realm that the rest of us cannot *see*? That, I must confess, would be *very* disappointing to me. Are they, as some scripture seems to suggest, burning in hell right now? That would work just fine for me. Of course, one corollary of the theory that evil people go to hell is the possibility that I will eventually *join* them there. That would also be *quite* disappointing to me. I hardly went to the time, trouble, and effort to kill these guys just so that I could burn along with them in eternal hellfire. That would be one hell of an awkward "reunion," would it not? I can only hope that such an experience is not in my future.

Time will tell.

What about my *family*, by the way? My wife was never particularly religious, and there are, of course, those who claim that people who lack faith, or who fail to engage in proper "works," end up in hell whether they are otherwise kind and gentle or not. Is my wife currently in the same place as Ed and Travis? That would be *far* worse than a mere disappointment for me. Surely, my wife could not be happy keeping company with *those* guys.

Epicurus said that, "Death is nothing to us, for when it *is*, we are *not*, and when we *are*, it is *not*," or something along those lines, anyway. If he is correct, then my family and my victims are *not*. They have *all* simply *ceased to exist*. Perhaps it is strange to say so, but I find that possibility oddly comforting, at least in *some* of my moods. Maybe my wife and family are nowhere at all, and my victims are also nowhere at all. In this instance, however, nowhere is *not* the *same* place in both cases. They have not all gone to a location called "nowhere," but rather they have not gone *anywhere* at all. They have been dispatched to nothingness. This *is* a possibility. It is preferable, I suppose, to imagining people I love in hell. If my wife and children no longer exist in *any* form at all, then they can no longer suffer, they can no longer experience fear, and they will never be victimized by anyone ever again. It may be that death is a *return* to nothingness. I cannot claim to *know* that this is *not* so. I will continue to hope that my family is in heaven, but I can live with the nothingness as well. What choice do I have in the matter?

It is a common belief, on the subject of death, that a person who dies while he is dreaming will die in reality. I can confidently report that this is *not* true or, at the very least, it is not true in *my* case. I have died in more dreams than I can count or recall. Some of these dreams are of the recurring variety. At least once a month, I dream that I am drowning, suffocating, or being strangled to death. In most cases, I do *not* escape. I *die* in the dream. Not only do I not die in reality, but I often do not even *wake* immediately from the dream. Everything goes black when I die in my dreams, but I often linger a long while in that blackness. My mind continues to think thoughts while I am dead in my dreams. Perhaps this is merely because my mind is still functioning in reality, outside of the dream, but it might also be an indication about what the mind does after *actual* bodily death, might it not? Maybe I have been granted a glimpse of the blackness that will be my lot after I die for real. If so, then it does not strike me as all that terrible, at least in *small* doses. An *eternity* in that blackness might become far more troubling over an infinite amount of time. It could lead to a kind of disembodied madness, I suppose. Maybe *that* is what *hell* is really all about. It might be an eternity locked in darkness alone within one's own relentlessly thinking mind. I do not know if hell is real. I suppose it *could* take that form.

What I *do* know is that my victims are dead. My family is dead. I, however, seem to go on living. This is something of a punishment in and of itself. My family and my victims also *all* visit me in my dreams. In *those* dreams, I do *not* die. Generally, I face recriminations from those I loved, and also from those whom I have killed. Nobody is particularly *happy* with me in those dreams. There are no reconciliations. We do *not* make peace with each other. Most of those who visit me in my dreams tell me about the terrible things I have done, and they often inform me of the various ways in which I am going to pay for my flawed character and evil deeds. For the most part, I tend to believe their predictions. I fully *expect* to pay for what I have done in one form or another.

Time will tell.

A Generous Tip

I am sitting at a diner in Sonora, CA. It is a quaint little place. My leather-bound journal is just about filled up at this point. I have been writing these final pages in the journal while eating my breakfast, and I have been lingering a bit, and writing more, as I drink what is left of my coffee. Probably, I should not linger here much longer. That might draw undesirable attention. That could be inconvenient. I do *not* like to be inconvenienced.

My breakfast cost just under twenty dollars. That is pretty expensive for one person, but inflation these days has gotten out of hand. There is not a great deal I can do about inflation, as far as I can tell. In any event, I have decided that I am going to leave forty dollars, a twenty and two ten-dollar bills, poking out from the middle of the pages of this journal. I am going to leave the journal on the table with the money in it, and then I will leave and never return to this place. There is *no* other copy of this memoir. I will put the book down here and walk away. What happens after *that* is difficult to predict with any confidence.

This is *not* a *smart* thing to do. I understand that. More than six months have passed since I killed Sam. His "suicide" is probably forgotten by everyone other than those who knew him well. Thus far, no police have knocked on my door. I have, it seems, "gotten away" with all of the crimes I have described here (so far, any rate). So, *why* would I leave the journal in this diner and risk someone reading it, "connecting a few dots," and possibly finding me?

As is so frequently the case with indefensibly stupid behavior, I think this comes down to the *ego*. The love of *self* is the real root of all evil and also an *awful* lot of stupidity. Criminals often get caught because they simply *cannot* keep their mouths shut about their misdeeds. I have always regarded this with a mixture of contempt and disbelief. How can they possibly be *that* stupid? Well, now I guess I have a bit more insight into that perspective. I suppose I *want* someone to know *what* I have done, but fervently hope that nobody will figure out *who* has done what I have done, or where anybody can *find* me. I still do *not* want to go to prison. Nevertheless, I *am* going to leave this collection of clues to my crimes on a table at a diner in a town I have never visited before, and one that I will never visit again. Something compels me, but I cannot explain that compulsion very well. Much of the human condition seems to be like that. It is difficult to explain *why* we do *what* we do.

It is probably inadvisable to return to the diner where I leave this collection of clues to my identity. It is, of course, also inadvisable to leave this collection of clues *anywhere*, and it is certainly contrary to my interests, particularly my interest in avoiding prison, to have written this memoir of my various criminal exploits in the first place. *Why* did I write this memoir at all? Perhaps my hope is that someone will read it and understand why I have done what I have done. Then again, I do not know that I really *want* to be understood. Certainly, I am not seeking absolution for killing terrible people. Only God has the power to absolve me, *if* God exists, and God does not need to *read* what I have written. If He exists, then He already knows everything. Maybe I am just seeking something like catharsis, but I do not know that I have gotten much of *that* from writing this account. I do not feel *purified* by what I have written. If anything, I feel *embarrassed*. I am not, after all, a talented writer. It might just be that everyone wants to tell their story, and *mine* happens to involve several murders. Understanding one's own motives is generally a difficult undertaking, after all. In any event, I am well aware that I might be contributing to my own downfall, and prison might be in my future because of what I have done and because of what I *am* doing *now*. If that is the result of this act, then I will accept my punishment with whatever equanimity I can muster. I cannot claim that I do *not* deserve to be imprisoned or executed for the crimes I have committed. Ultimately, I suppose I am leaving this account of my deeds in this diner for the same reason that I have killed the people mentioned in this memoir. I suppose I am doing it simply because I *want* to do it. *Why* I want *what* I want remains somewhat unclear to me. I am a bit of a mystery to myself. How could it be otherwise? All I can say for certain is that I identified some people who, in my judgment, *needed* killing, and I killed a few of them. What anyone *else* might make of my actions is, of course, not up to me.

If I *am* caught, then I *will* confess to everything. There is no need to subject myself, the attorneys, a judge, or a jury to the charade of a trial. I readily admit that I am guilty of killing some genuinely terrible men. As far as the laws of man are concerned, I *am* a murderer. Will I be compelled to pay for these crimes? Anybody else can predict the future about as well as I can manage. Who knows?

Of course, it is also possible that the waitress who has filled and refilled my coffee several times by now will pull the money out of the journal, never open the book or look inside, and just toss this memoir into the trash along with my napkins and the remains of my eggs and hashbrowns. Maybe the book will end up undetected in a dumpster. Maybe it will end up like Travis' body in that respect. It is possible that everything I have written here will simply find its way to a landfill, and nobody will ever read a word of it.

Time will tell.

ROUNDFIRE
BOOKS

FICTION

Put simply, we publish great stories. Whether it's literary or
popular, a gentle tale or a pulsating thriller, the connecting theme
in all Roundfire fiction titles is that once you pick them up you
won't want to put them down.
If you have enjoyed this book, why not tell other readers by
posting a review on your preferred book site.

The Cause

Roderick Vincent

The second American Revolution will be a
fire lit from an internal spark.

Paperback: 978-1-78279-763-0 ebook: 978-1-78279-762-3

Don't Drink and Fly

The Story of Bernice O'Hanlon: Part One

Cathie Devitt

Bernice is a witch living in Glasgow. She loses her way
in her life and wanders off the beaten track looking for the
garden of enlightenment.

Paperback: 978-1-78279-016-7 ebook: 978-1-78279-015-0

Gag

Melissa Unger

One rainy afternoon in a Brooklyn diner, Peter Howland
punctures an egg with his fork. Repulsed, Peter pushes
the plate away and never eats again.

Paperback: 978-1-78279-564-3 ebook: 978-1-78279-563-6

The Master Yeshua

The Undiscovered Gospel of Joseph

Joyce Luck

Jesus is not who you think he is. The year is 75 CE. Joseph
ben Jude is frail and ailing, but he has a prophecy to fulfil ...

Paperback: 978-1-78279-974-0 ebook: 978-1-78279-975-7

On the Far Side, There's a Boy
Paula Coston

Martine Haslett, a thirty-something 1980s woman, plays hard on the fringes of the London drag club scene until one night which prompts her to sign up to a charity. She writes to a young Sri Lankan boy, with consequences far and long.
Paperback: 978-1-78279-574-2 ebook: 978-1-78279-573-5

Tuareg
Alberto Vazquez-Figueroa

With over 5 million copies sold worldwide, *Tuareg* is a classic adventure story from best-selling author Alberto Vazquez-Figueroa, about honour, revenge and a clash of cultures.
Paperback: 978-1-84694-192-4

Readers of ebooks can buy or view any of these bestsellers by clicking on the live link in the title. Most titles are published in paperback and as an ebook. Paperbacks are available in traditional bookshops. Both print and ebook formats are available online.

Find more titles and sign up to our readers' newsletter at www.collectiveinkbooks.com/fiction